HAMLET

WILLIAM SHAKESPEARE

CRICKET
HOUSE
BOOKS

PERSONS REPRESENTED

Claudius, KING of Denmark

HAMLET, son to the former, and nephew to the present
    King Claudius

POLONIUS, Lord Chamberlain

HORATIO, friend to Hamlet

LAERTES, son to Polonius

VOLTIMAND, courtier

CORNELIUS, courtier

ROSENCRANTZ, courtier

GUILDENSTERN, courtier

OSRIC, courtier

A GENTLEMAN, courtier

A PRIEST

MARCELLUS, officer

BERNARDO, officer

FRANCISCO, a soldier

REYNALDO, servant to Polonius

PLAYERS

Two CLOWNS, grave-diggers

FORTINBRAS, Prince of Norway

A CAPTAIN

English AMBASSADORS

GHOST of Hamlet's father

Gertrude, QUEEN of Denmark, and mother of Hamlet

OPHELIA, daughter to Polonius

Lords, Ladies, Officers, Soldiers, Sailors, Messengers,
    and other Attendants

ACT I

Scene I. Elsinore. A platform before the Castle.

[Francisco at his post. Enter to him Bernardo.]

BERNARDO
Who's there?

FRANCISCO
Nay, answer me: stand, and unfold yourself.

BERNARDO
Long live the king!

FRANCISCO
Bernardo?

BERNARDO
He.

FRANCISCO
You come most carefully upon your hour.

BERNARDO
'Tis now struck twelve. Get thee to bed, Francisco.

FRANCISCO
For this relief much thanks: 'tis bitter cold,
And I am sick at heart.

BERNARDO
Have you had quiet guard?

FRANCISCO
Not a mouse stirring.

BERNARDO
Well, good night.
If you do meet Horatio and Marcellus,
The rivals of my watch, bid them make haste.

FRANCISCO
I think I hear them.—Stand, ho! Who is there?

[Enter Horatio and Marcellus.]

HORATIO
Friends to this ground.

MARCELLUS
And liegemen to the Dane.

FRANCISCO
Give you good-night.

MARCELLUS
O, farewell, honest soldier;
Who hath reliev'd you?

FRANCISCO
Bernardo has my place.
Give you good-night.

[Exit.]

MARCELLUS
Holla! Bernardo!

BERNARDO
Say.
What, is Horatio there?

HORATIO
A piece of him.

BERNARDO
Welcome, Horatio:—Welcome, good Marcellus.

MARCELLUS
What, has this thing appear'd again to-night?

BERNARDO
I have seen nothing.

MARCELLUS
Horatio says 'tis but our fantasy,
And will not let belief take hold of him

Touching this dreaded sight, twice seen of us:
Therefore I have entreated him along
With us to watch the minutes of this night;
That, if again this apparition come
He may approve our eyes and speak to it.

HORATIO
Tush, tush, 'twill not appear.

BERNARDO
Sit down awhile,
And let us once again assail your ears,
That are so fortified against our story,
What we two nights have seen.

HORATIO
Well, sit we down,
And let us hear Bernardo speak of this.

BERNARDO
Last night of all,
When yond same star that's westward from the pole
Had made his course to illume that part of heaven
Where now it burns, Marcellus and myself,
The bell then beating one,—

MARCELLUS
Peace, break thee off; look where it comes again!

[Enter Ghost, armed.]

BERNARDO
In the same figure, like the king that's dead.

MARCELLUS
Thou art a scholar; speak to it, Horatio.

BERNARDO
Looks it not like the King? mark it, Horatio.

HORATIO
Most like:—it harrows me with fear and wonder.

BERNARDO
It would be spoke to.

MARCELLUS
Question it, Horatio.

HORATIO
What art thou, that usurp'st this time of night,
Together with that fair and warlike form
In which the majesty of buried Denmark
Did sometimes march? By heaven I charge thee, speak!

MARCELLUS
It is offended.

BERNARDO
See, it stalks away!

HORATIO
Stay! speak, speak! I charge thee speak!

[Exit Ghost.]

MARCELLUS
'Tis gone, and will not answer.

BERNARDO
How now, Horatio! You tremble and look pale:
Is not this something more than fantasy?
What think you on't?

HORATIO
Before my God, I might not this believe
Without the sensible and true avouch
Of mine own eyes.

MARCELLUS
Is it not like the King?

HORATIO
As thou art to thyself:
Such was the very armour he had on

When he the ambitious Norway combated;
So frown'd he once when, in an angry parle,
He smote the sledded Polacks on the ice.
'Tis strange.

MARCELLUS
Thus twice before, and jump at this dead hour,
With martial stalk hath he gone by our watch.

HORATIO
In what particular thought to work I know not;
But, in the gross and scope of my opinion,
This bodes some strange eruption to our state.

MARCELLUS
Good now, sit down, and tell me, he that knows,
Why this same strict and most observant watch
So nightly toils the subject of the land;
And why such daily cast of brazen cannon,
And foreign mart for implements of war;
Why such impress of shipwrights, whose sore task
Does not divide the Sunday from the week;
What might be toward, that this sweaty haste
Doth make the night joint-labourer with the day:
Who is't that can inform me?

HORATIO
That can I;
At least, the whisper goes so. Our last king,
Whose image even but now appear'd to us,
Was, as you know, by Fortinbras of Norway,
Thereto prick'd on by a most emulate pride,
Dar'd to the combat; in which our valiant Hamlet,—
For so this side of our known world esteem'd him,—
Did slay this Fortinbras; who, by a seal'd compact,
Well ratified by law and heraldry,
Did forfeit, with his life, all those his lands,
Which he stood seiz'd of, to the conqueror:

Against the which, a moiety competent
Was gaged by our king; which had return'd
To the inheritance of Fortinbras,
Had he been vanquisher; as by the same cov'nant,
And carriage of the article design'd,
His fell to Hamlet. Now, sir, young Fortinbras,
Of unimproved mettle hot and full,
Hath in the skirts of Norway, here and there,
Shark'd up a list of lawless resolutes,
For food and diet, to some enterprise
That hath a stomach in't; which is no other,—
As it doth well appear unto our state,—
But to recover of us, by strong hand,
And terms compulsatory, those foresaid lands
So by his father lost: and this, I take it,
Is the main motive of our preparations,
The source of this our watch, and the chief head
Of this post-haste and romage in the land.

BERNARDO
I think it be no other but e'en so:
Well may it sort, that this portentous figure
Comes armed through our watch; so like the king
That was and is the question of these wars.

HORATIO
A mote it is to trouble the mind's eye.
In the most high and palmy state of Rome,
A little ere the mightiest Julius fell,
The graves stood tenantless, and the sheeted dead
Did squeak and gibber in the Roman streets;
As, stars with trains of fire and dews of blood,
Disasters in the sun; and the moist star,
Upon whose influence Neptune's empire stands,
Was sick almost to doomsday with eclipse:
And even the like precurse of fierce events,—
As harbingers preceding still the fates,

And prologue to the omen coming on,—
Have heaven and earth together demonstrated
Unto our climature and countrymen.—
But, soft, behold! lo, where it comes again!

[Re-enter Ghost.]

I'll cross it, though it blast me.—Stay, illusion!
If thou hast any sound, or use of voice,
Speak to me:
If there be any good thing to be done,
That may to thee do ease, and, race to me,
Speak to me:
If thou art privy to thy country's fate,
Which, happily, foreknowing may avoid,
O, speak!
Or if thou hast uphoarded in thy life
Extorted treasure in the womb of earth,
For which, they say, you spirits oft walk in death,
[The cock crows.]
Speak of it:—stay, and speak!—Stop it, Marcellus!

MARCELLUS
Shall I strike at it with my partisan?

HORATIO
Do, if it will not stand.

BERNARDO
'Tis here!

HORATIO
'Tis here!

MARCELLUS
'Tis gone!

[Exit Ghost.]

We do it wrong, being so majestical,
To offer it the show of violence;

For it is, as the air, invulnerable,
And our vain blows malicious mockery.

BERNARDO
It was about to speak, when the cock crew.

HORATIO
And then it started, like a guilty thing
Upon a fearful summons. I have heard
The cock, that is the trumpet to the morn,
Doth with his lofty and shrill-sounding throat
Awake the god of day; and at his warning,
Whether in sea or fire, in earth or air,
The extravagant and erring spirit hies
To his confine: and of the truth herein
This present object made probation.

MARCELLUS
It faded on the crowing of the cock.
Some say that ever 'gainst that season comes
Wherein our Saviour's birth is celebrated,
The bird of dawning singeth all night long;
And then, they say, no spirit dare stir abroad;
The nights are wholesome; then no planets strike,
No fairy takes, nor witch hath power to charm;
So hallow'd and so gracious is the time.

HORATIO
So have I heard, and do in part believe it.
But, look, the morn, in russet mantle clad,
Walks o'er the dew of yon high eastward hill:
Break we our watch up: and by my advice,
Let us impart what we have seen to-night
Unto young Hamlet; for, upon my life,
This spirit, dumb to us, will speak to him:
Do you consent we shall acquaint him with it,
As needful in our loves, fitting our duty?

MARCELLUS
Let's do't, I pray; and I this morning know
Where we shall find him most conveniently.

[Exeunt.]

Scene II. Elsinore. A room of state in the Castle.

[Enter the King, Queen, Hamlet, Polonius, Laertes, Voltimand, Cornelius, Lords, and Attendant.]

KING
Though yet of Hamlet our dear brother's death
The memory be green, and that it us befitted
To bear our hearts in grief, and our whole kingdom
To be contracted in one brow of woe;
Yet so far hath discretion fought with nature
That we with wisest sorrow think on him,
Together with remembrance of ourselves.
Therefore our sometime sister, now our queen,
Th' imperial jointress to this warlike state,
Have we, as 'twere with a defeated joy,—
With an auspicious and one dropping eye,
With mirth in funeral, and with dirge in marriage,
In equal scale weighing delight and dole,—
Taken to wife; nor have we herein barr'd
Your better wisdoms, which have freely gone
With this affair along:—or all, our thanks.
Now follows, that you know, young Fortinbras,
Holding a weak supposal of our worth,
Or thinking by our late dear brother's death
Our state to be disjoint and out of frame,
Colleagued with this dream of his advantage,
He hath not fail'd to pester us with message,
Importing the surrender of those lands
Lost by his father, with all bonds of law,
To our most valiant brother. So much for him,—
Now for ourself and for this time of meeting:

Thus much the business is:—we have here writ
To Norway, uncle of young Fortinbras,—
Who, impotent and bed-rid, scarcely hears
Of this his nephew's purpose,—to suppress
His further gait herein; in that the levies,
The lists, and full proportions are all made
Out of his subject:—and we here dispatch
You, good Cornelius, and you, Voltimand,
For bearers of this greeting to old Norway;
Giving to you no further personal power
To business with the king, more than the scope
Of these dilated articles allow.
Farewell; and let your haste commend your duty.

CORNELIUS AND VOLTIMAND
In that and all things will we show our duty.

KING
We doubt it nothing: heartily farewell.

[Exeunt Voltimand and Cornelius.]

And now, Laertes, what's the news with you?
You told us of some suit; what is't, Laertes?
You cannot speak of reason to the Dane,
And lose your voice: what wouldst thou beg, Laertes,
That shall not be my offer, not thy asking?
The head is not more native to the heart,
The hand more instrumental to the mouth,
Than is the throne of Denmark to thy father.
What wouldst thou have, Laertes?

LAERTES
Dread my lord,
Your leave and favour to return to France;
From whence though willingly I came to Denmark,
To show my duty in your coronation;
Yet now, I must confess, that duty done,
My thoughts and wishes bend again toward France,
And bow them to your gracious leave and pardon.

KING

Have you your father's leave? What says Polonius?

POLONIUS

He hath, my lord, wrung from me my slow leave
By laboursome petition; and at last
Upon his will I seal'd my hard consent:
I do beseech you, give him leave to go.

KING

Take thy fair hour, Laertes; time be thine,
And thy best graces spend it at thy will!—
But now, my cousin Hamlet, and my son—

HAMLET

[Aside.] A little more than kin, and less than kind!

KING

How is it that the clouds still hang on you?

HAMLET

Not so, my lord; I am too much i' the sun.

QUEEN

Good Hamlet, cast thy nighted colour off,
And let thine eye look like a friend on Denmark.
Do not for ever with thy vailed lids
Seek for thy noble father in the dust:
Thou know'st 'tis common,—all that lives must die,
Passing through nature to eternity.

HAMLET

Ay, madam, it is common.

QUEEN

If it be,
Why seems it so particular with thee?

HAMLET

Seems, madam! Nay, it is; I know not seems.
'Tis not alone my inky cloak, good mother,

Nor customary suits of solemn black,
Nor windy suspiration of forc'd breath,
No, nor the fruitful river in the eye,
Nor the dejected 'havior of the visage,
Together with all forms, moods, shows of grief,
That can denote me truly: these, indeed, seem;
For they are actions that a man might play;
But I have that within which passeth show;
These but the trappings and the suits of woe.

KING
'Tis sweet and commendable in your nature, Hamlet,
To give these mourning duties to your father;
But, you must know, your father lost a father;
That father lost, lost his; and the survivor bound,
In filial obligation, for some term
To do obsequious sorrow: but to persevere
In obstinate condolement is a course
Of impious stubbornness; 'tis unmanly grief;
It shows a will most incorrect to heaven;
A heart unfortified, a mind impatient;
An understanding simple and unschool'd;
For what we know must be, and is as common
As any the most vulgar thing to sense,
Why should we, in our peevish opposition,
Take it to heart? Fie! 'tis a fault to heaven,
A fault against the dead, a fault to nature,
To reason most absurd; whose common theme
Is death of fathers, and who still hath cried,
From the first corse till he that died to-day,
'This must be so.' We pray you, throw to earth
This unprevailing woe; and think of us
As of a father: for let the world take note
You are the most immediate to our throne;
And with no less nobility of love
Than that which dearest father bears his son
Do I impart toward you. For your intent

In going back to school in Wittenberg,
It is most retrograde to our desire:
And we beseech you bend you to remain
Here in the cheer and comfort of our eye,
Our chiefest courtier, cousin, and our son.

QUEEN
Let not thy mother lose her prayers, Hamlet:
I pray thee stay with us; go not to Wittenberg.

HAMLET
I shall in all my best obey you, madam.

KING
Why, 'tis a loving and a fair reply:
Be as ourself in Denmark.—Madam, come;
This gentle and unforc'd accord of Hamlet
Sits smiling to my heart: in grace whereof,
No jocund health that Denmark drinks to-day
But the great cannon to the clouds shall tell;
And the king's rouse the heaven shall bruit again,
Re-speaking earthly thunder. Come away.

[Exeunt all but Hamlet.]

HAMLET
O that this too too solid flesh would melt,
Thaw, and resolve itself into a dew!
Or that the Everlasting had not fix'd
His canon 'gainst self-slaughter! O God! O God!
How weary, stale, flat, and unprofitable
Seem to me all the uses of this world!
Fie on't! O fie! 'tis an unweeded garden,
That grows to seed; things rank and gross in nature
Possess it merely. That it should come to this!
But two months dead!—nay, not so much, not two:
So excellent a king; that was, to this,
Hyperion to a satyr; so loving to my mother,
That he might not beteem the winds of heaven

Visit her face too roughly. Heaven and earth!
Must I remember? Why, she would hang on him
As if increase of appetite had grown
By what it fed on: and yet, within a month,—
Let me not think on't,—Frailty, thy name is woman!—
A little month; or ere those shoes were old
With which she followed my poor father's body
Like Niobe, all tears;—why she, even she,—
O God! a beast that wants discourse of reason,
Would have mourn'd longer,—married with mine uncle,
My father's brother; but no more like my father
Than I to Hercules: within a month;
Ere yet the salt of most unrighteous tears
Had left the flushing in her galled eyes,
She married:— O, most wicked speed, to post
With such dexterity to incestuous sheets!
It is not, nor it cannot come to good;
But break my heart,—for I must hold my tongue!

[Enter Horatio, Marcellus, and Bernardo.]

HORATIO
Hail to your lordship!

HAMLET
I am glad to see you well:
Horatio,—or I do forget myself.

HORATIO
The same, my lord, and your poor servant ever.

HAMLET
Sir, my good friend; I'll change that name with you:
And what make you from Wittenberg, Horatio?—
Marcellus?

MARCELLUS
My good lord,—

HAMLET
I am very glad to see you.—Good even, sir.—
But what, in faith, make you from Wittenberg?

HORATIO
A truant disposition, good my lord.

HAMLET
I would not hear your enemy say so;
Nor shall you do my ear that violence,
To make it truster of your own report
Against yourself: I know you are no truant.
But what is your affair in Elsinore?
We'll teach you to drink deep ere you depart.

HORATIO
My lord, I came to see your father's funeral.

HAMLET
I prithee do not mock me, fellow-student.
I think it was to see my mother's wedding.

HORATIO
Indeed, my lord, it follow'd hard upon.

HAMLET
Thrift, thrift, Horatio! The funeral bak'd meats
Did coldly furnish forth the marriage tables.
Would I had met my dearest foe in heaven
Or ever I had seen that day, Horatio!—
My father,—methinks I see my father.

HORATIO
Where, my lord?

HAMLET
In my mind's eye, Horatio.

HORATIO
I saw him once; he was a goodly king.

HAMLET
He was a man, take him for all in all,
I shall not look upon his like again.

HORATIO
My lord, I think I saw him yesternight.

HAMLET
Saw who?

HORATIO
My lord, the king your father.

HAMLET
The King my father!

HORATIO
Season your admiration for awhile
With an attent ear, till I may deliver,
Upon the witness of these gentlemen,
This marvel to you.

HAMLET
For God's love let me hear.

HORATIO
Two nights together had these gentlemen,
Marcellus and Bernardo, on their watch
In the dead vast and middle of the night,
Been thus encounter'd. A figure like your father,
Armed at point exactly, cap-a-pe,
Appears before them and with solemn march
Goes slow and stately by them: thrice he walk'd
By their oppress'd and fear-surprised eyes,
Within his truncheon's length; whilst they, distill'd
Almost to jelly with the act of fear,
Stand dumb, and speak not to him. This to me
In dreadful secrecy impart they did;
And I with them the third night kept the watch:
Where, as they had deliver'd, both in time,

Form of the thing, each word made true and good,
The apparition comes: I knew your father;
These hands are not more like.

HAMLET
But where was this?

MARCELLUS
My lord, upon the platform where we watch'd.

HAMLET
Did you not speak to it?

HORATIO
My lord, I did;
But answer made it none: yet once methought
It lifted up it head, and did address
Itself to motion, like as it would speak:
But even then the morning cock crew loud,
And at the sound it shrunk in haste away,
And vanish'd from our sight.

HAMLET
'Tis very strange.

HORATIO
As I do live, my honour'd lord, 'tis true;
And we did think it writ down in our duty
To let you know of it.

HAMLET
Indeed, indeed, sirs, but this troubles me.
Hold you the watch to-night?

MARCELLUS AND BERNARDO
We do, my lord.

HAMLET
Arm'd, say you?

BOTH
Arm'd, my lord.

HAMLET
From top to toe?

BOTH
My lord, from head to foot.

HAMLET
Then saw you not his face?

HORATIO
O, yes, my lord: he wore his beaver up.

HAMLET
What, look'd he frowningly?

HORATIO
A countenance more in sorrow than in anger.

HAMLET
Pale or red?

HORATIO
Nay, very pale.

HAMLET
And fix'd his eyes upon you?

HORATIO
Most constantly.

HAMLET
I would I had been there.

HORATIO
It would have much amaz'd you.

HAMLET
Very like, very like. Stay'd it long?

HORATIO
While one with moderate haste might tell a hundred.

MARCELLUS AND BERNARDO
Longer, longer.

HORATIO
Not when I saw't.

HAMLET
His beard was grizzled,—no?

HORATIO
It was, as I have seen it in his life,
A sable silver'd.

HAMLET
I will watch to-night;
Perchance 'twill walk again.

HORATIO
I warr'nt it will.

HAMLET
If it assume my noble father's person,
I'll speak to it, though hell itself should gape
And bid me hold my peace. I pray you all,
If you have hitherto conceal'd this sight,
Let it be tenable in your silence still;
And whatsoever else shall hap to-night,
Give it an understanding, but no tongue:
I will requite your loves. So, fare ye well:
Upon the platform, 'twixt eleven and twelve,
I'll visit you.

ALL
Our duty to your honour.

HAMLET
Your loves, as mine to you: farewell.

[Exeunt Horatio, Marcellus, and Bernardo.]

My father's spirit in arms! All is not well;
I doubt some foul play: would the night were come!
Till then sit still, my soul: foul deeds will rise,
Though all the earth o'erwhelm them, to men's eyes.

[Exit.]

Scene III. A room in Polonius's house.

[Enter Laertes and Ophelia.]

LAERTES
My necessaries are embark'd: farewell:
And, sister, as the winds give benefit
And convoy is assistant, do not sleep,
But let me hear from you.

OPHELIA
Do you doubt that?

LAERTES
For Hamlet, and the trifling of his favour,
Hold it a fashion, and a toy in blood:
A violet in the youth of primy nature,
Forward, not permanent, sweet, not lasting;
The perfume and suppliance of a minute;
No more.

OPHELIA
No more but so?

LAERTES
Think it no more:
For nature, crescent, does not grow alone
In thews and bulk; but as this temple waxes,
The inward service of the mind and soul
Grows wide withal. Perhaps he loves you now;
And now no soil nor cautel doth besmirch
The virtue of his will: but you must fear,
His greatness weigh'd, his will is not his own;
For he himself is subject to his birth:
He may not, as unvalu'd persons do,
Carve for himself; for on his choice depends
The safety and health of this whole state;
And therefore must his choice be circumscrib'd

Unto the voice and yielding of that body
Whereof he is the head. Then if he says he loves you,
It fits your wisdom so far to believe it
As he in his particular act and place
May give his saying deed; which is no further
Than the main voice of Denmark goes withal.
Then weigh what loss your honour may sustain
If with too credent ear you list his songs,
Or lose your heart, or your chaste treasure open
To his unmaster'd importunity.
Fear it, Ophelia, fear it, my dear sister;
And keep you in the rear of your affection,
Out of the shot and danger of desire.
The chariest maid is prodigal enough
If she unmask her beauty to the moon:
Virtue itself scopes not calumnious strokes:
The canker galls the infants of the spring
Too oft before their buttons be disclos'd:
And in the morn and liquid dew of youth
Contagious blastments are most imminent.
Be wary then; best safety lies in fear:
Youth to itself rebels, though none else near.

OPHELIA
I shall th' effect of this good lesson keep
As watchman to my heart. But, good my brother,
Do not, as some ungracious pastors do,
Show me the steep and thorny way to heaven;
Whilst, like a puff'd and reckless libertine,
Himself the primrose path of dalliance treads
And recks not his own read.

LAERTES
O, fear me not.
I stay too long:—but here my father comes.

[Enter Polonius.]

A double blessing is a double grace;
Occasion smiles upon a second leave.

POLONIUS
Yet here, Laertes! aboard, aboard, for shame!
The wind sits in the shoulder of your sail,
And you are stay'd for. There,—my blessing with thee!

[Laying his hand on Laertes's head.]

And these few precepts in thy memory
Look thou character. Give thy thoughts no tongue,
Nor any unproportion'd thought his act.
Be thou familiar, but by no means vulgar.
Those friends thou hast, and their adoption tried,
Grapple them unto thy soul with hoops of steel;
But do not dull thy palm with entertainment
Of each new-hatch'd, unfledg'd comrade. Beware
Of entrance to a quarrel; but, being in,
Bear't that the opposed may beware of thee.
Give every man thine ear, but few thy voice:
Take each man's censure, but reserve thy judgment.
Costly thy habit as thy purse can buy,
But not express'd in fancy; rich, not gaudy:
For the apparel oft proclaims the man;
And they in France of the best rank and station
Are most select and generous chief in that.
Neither a borrower nor a lender be:
For loan oft loses both itself and friend;
And borrowing dulls the edge of husbandry.
This above all,—to thine own self be true;
And it must follow, as the night the day,
Thou canst not then be false to any man.
Farewell: my blessing season this in thee!

LAERTES
Most humbly do I take my leave, my lord.

POLONIUS
The time invites you; go, your servants tend.

LAERTES
Farewell, Ophelia; and remember well
What I have said to you.

OPHELIA
'Tis in my memory lock'd,
And you yourself shall keep the key of it.

LAERTES
Farewell.

[Exit.]

POLONIUS
What is't, Ophelia, he hath said to you?

OPHELIA
So please you, something touching the Lord Hamlet.

POLONIUS
Marry, well bethought:
'Tis told me he hath very oft of late
Given private time to you; and you yourself
Have of your audience been most free and bounteous;
If it be so,—as so 'tis put on me,
And that in way of caution,—I must tell you
You do not understand yourself so clearly
As it behooves my daughter and your honour.
What is between you? give me up the truth.

OPHELIA
He hath, my lord, of late made many tenders
Of his affection to me.

POLONIUS
Affection! pooh! you speak like a green girl,
Unsifted in such perilous circumstance.
Do you believe his tenders, as you call them?

OPHELIA
I do not know, my lord, what I should think.

POLONIUS

Marry, I'll teach you: think yourself a baby;
That you have ta'en these tenders for true pay,
Which are not sterling. Tender yourself more dearly;
Or,—not to crack the wind of the poor phrase,
Wronging it thus,—you'll tender me a fool.

OPHELIA

My lord, he hath importun'd me with love
In honourable fashion.

POLONIUS

Ay, fashion you may call it; go to, go to.

OPHELIA

And hath given countenance to his speech, my lord,
With almost all the holy vows of heaven.

POLONIUS

Ay, springes to catch woodcocks. I do know,
When the blood burns, how prodigal the soul
Lends the tongue vows: these blazes, daughter,
Giving more light than heat,—extinct in both,
Even in their promise, as it is a-making,—
You must not take for fire. From this time
Be something scanter of your maiden presence;
Set your entreatments at a higher rate
Than a command to parley. For Lord Hamlet,
Believe so much in him, that he is young;
And with a larger tether may he walk
Than may be given you: in few, Ophelia,
Do not believe his vows; for they are brokers,—
Not of that dye which their investments show,
But mere implorators of unholy suits,
Breathing like sanctified and pious bawds,
The better to beguile. This is for all,—
I would not, in plain terms, from this time forth
Have you so slander any moment leisure

As to give words or talk with the Lord Hamlet.
Look to't, I charge you; come your ways.

OPHELIA
I shall obey, my lord.

[Exeunt.]

Scene IV. The platform.

[Enter Hamlet, Horatio, and Marcellus.]

HAMLET
The air bites shrewdly; it is very cold.

HORATIO
It is a nipping and an eager air.

HAMLET
What hour now?

HORATIO
I think it lacks of twelve.

MARCELLUS
No, it is struck.

HORATIO
Indeed? I heard it not: then draws near the season
Wherein the spirit held his wont to walk.

[A flourish of trumpets, and ordnance shot off within.]

What does this mean, my lord?

HAMLET
The King doth wake to-night and takes his rouse,
Keeps wassail, and the swaggering up-spring reels;
And, as he drains his draughts of Rhenish down,
The kettle-drum and trumpet thus bray out
The triumph of his pledge.

HORATIO
Is it a custom?

HAMLET
Ay, marry, is't;
But to my mind,—though I am native here,
And to the manner born,—it is a custom
More honour'd in the breach than the observance.
This heavy-headed revel east and west
Makes us traduc'd and tax'd of other nations:
They clepe us drunkards, and with swinish phrase
Soil our addition; and, indeed, it takes
From our achievements, though perform'd at height,
The pith and marrow of our attribute.
So oft it chances in particular men
That, for some vicious mole of nature in them,
As in their birth,—wherein they are not guilty,
Since nature cannot choose his origin,—
By the o'ergrowth of some complexion,
Oft breaking down the pales and forts of reason;
Or by some habit, that too much o'er-leavens
The form of plausive manners;—that these men,—
Carrying, I say, the stamp of one defect,
Being nature's livery, or fortune's star,—
Their virtues else,—be they as pure as grace,
As infinite as man may undergo,—
Shall in the general censure take corruption
From that particular fault: the dram of eale
Doth all the noble substance often doubt
To his own scandal.

HORATIO
Look, my lord, it comes!

[Enter Ghost.]

HAMLET
Angels and ministers of grace defend us!—
Be thou a spirit of health or goblin damn'd,
Bring with thee airs from heaven or blasts from hell,
Be thy intents wicked or charitable,

Thou com'st in such a questionable shape
That I will speak to thee: I'll call thee Hamlet,
King, father, royal Dane; O, answer me!
Let me not burst in ignorance; but tell
Why thy canoniz'd bones, hearsed in death,
Have burst their cerements; why the sepulchre,
Wherein we saw thee quietly in-urn'd,
Hath op'd his ponderous and marble jaws
To cast thee up again! What may this mean,
That thou, dead corse, again in complete steel,
Revisit'st thus the glimpses of the moon,
Making night hideous, and we fools of nature
So horridly to shake our disposition
With thoughts beyond the reaches of our souls?
Say, why is this? wherefore? what should we do?

[Ghost beckons Hamlet.]

HORATIO
It beckons you to go away with it,
As if it some impartment did desire
To you alone.

MARCELLUS
Look with what courteous action
It waves you to a more removed ground:
But do not go with it!

HORATIO
No, by no means.

HAMLET
It will not speak; then will I follow it.

HORATIO
Do not, my lord.

HAMLET
Why, what should be the fear?
I do not set my life at a pin's fee;

And for my soul, what can it do to that,
Being a thing immortal as itself?
It waves me forth again;—I'll follow it.

HORATIO
What if it tempt you toward the flood, my lord,
Or to the dreadful summit of the cliff
That beetles o'er his base into the sea,
And there assume some other horrible form
Which might deprive your sovereignty of reason,
And draw you into madness? think of it:
The very place puts toys of desperation,
Without more motive, into every brain
That looks so many fadoms to the sea
And hears it roar beneath.

HAMLET
It waves me still.—
Go on; I'll follow thee.

MARCELLUS
You shall not go, my lord.

HAMLET
Hold off your hands.

HORATIO
Be rul'd; you shall not go.

HAMLET
My fate cries out,
And makes each petty artery in this body
As hardy as the Nemean lion's nerve.—

[Ghost beckons.]

Still am I call'd;—unhand me, gentlemen;—

[Breaking free from them.]

By heaven, I'll make a ghost of him that lets me!—
I say, away!—Go on; I'll follow thee.

[Exeunt Ghost and Hamlet.]

HORATIO
He waxes desperate with imagination.

MARCELLUS
Let's follow; 'tis not fit thus to obey him.

HORATIO
Have after.—To what issue will this come?

MARCELLUS
Something is rotten in the state of Denmark.

HORATIO
Heaven will direct it.

MARCELLUS
Nay, let's follow him.

[Exeunt.]

Scene V. A more remote part of the Castle.

[Enter Ghost and Hamlet.]

HAMLET
Whither wilt thou lead me? speak! I'll go no further.

GHOST
Mark me.

HAMLET
I will.

GHOST
My hour is almost come,
When I to sulph'uous and tormenting flames
Must render up myself.

HAMLET
Alas, poor ghost!

GHOST
Pity me not, but lend thy serious hearing
To what I shall unfold.

HAMLET
Speak; I am bound to hear.

GHOST
So art thou to revenge, when thou shalt hear.

HAMLET
What?

GHOST
I am thy father's spirit;
Doom'd for a certain term to walk the night,
And for the day confin'd to wastein fires,
Till the foul crimes done in my days of nature
Are burnt and purg'd away. But that I am forbid
To tell the secrets of my prison-house,
I could a tale unfold whose lightest word
Would harrow up thy soul; freeze thy young blood;
Make thy two eyes, like stars, start from their spheres;
Thy knotted and combined locks to part,
And each particular hair to stand on end
Like quills upon the fretful porcupine:
But this eternal blazon must not be
To ears of flesh and blood.—List, list, O, list!—
If thou didst ever thy dear father love—

HAMLET
O God!

GHOST
Revenge his foul and most unnatural murder.

HAMLET
Murder!

GHOST
Murder most foul, as in the best it is;
But this most foul, strange, and unnatural.

HAMLET
Haste me to know't, that I, with wings as swift
As meditation or the thoughts of love,
May sweep to my revenge.

GHOST
I find thee apt;
And duller shouldst thou be than the fat weed
That rots itself in ease on Lethe wharf,
Wouldst thou not stir in this. Now, Hamlet, hear.
'Tis given out that, sleeping in my orchard,
A serpent stung me; so the whole ear of Denmark
Is by a forged process of my death
Rankly abus'd; but know, thou noble youth,
The serpent that did sting thy father's life
Now wears his crown.

HAMLET
O my prophetic soul!
Mine uncle!

GHOST
Ay, that incestuous, that adulterate beast,
With witchcraft of his wit, with traitorous gifts,—
O wicked wit and gifts, that have the power
So to seduce!—won to his shameful lust
The will of my most seeming-virtuous queen:
O Hamlet, what a falling-off was there!
From me, whose love was of that dignity
That it went hand in hand even with the vow
I made to her in marriage; and to decline
Upon a wretch whose natural gifts were poor
To those of mine!
But virtue, as it never will be mov'd,

Though lewdness court it in a shape of heaven;
So lust, though to a radiant angel link'd,
Will sate itself in a celestial bed
And prey on garbage.
But soft! methinks I scent the morning air;
Brief let me be.—Sleeping within my orchard,
My custom always of the afternoon,
Upon my secure hour thy uncle stole,
With juice of cursed hebenon in a vial,
And in the porches of my ears did pour
The leperous distilment; whose effect
Holds such an enmity with blood of man
That, swift as quicksilver, it courses through
The natural gates and alleys of the body;
And with a sudden vigour it doth posset
And curd, like eager droppings into milk,
The thin and wholesome blood; so did it mine;
And a most instant tetter bark'd about,
Most lazar-like, with vile and loathsome crust
All my smooth body.
Thus was I, sleeping, by a brother's hand,
Of life, of crown, of queen, at once dispatch'd:
Cut off even in the blossoms of my sin,
Unhous'led, disappointed, unanel'd;
No reckoning made, but sent to my account
With all my imperfections on my head:
O, horrible! O, horrible! most horrible!
If thou hast nature in thee, bear it not;
Let not the royal bed of Denmark be
A couch for luxury and damned incest.
But, howsoever thou pursu'st this act,
Taint not thy mind, nor let thy soul contrive
Against thy mother aught: leave her to heaven,
And to those thorns that in her bosom lodge,
To prick and sting her. Fare thee well at once!
The glowworm shows the matin to be near,

And 'gins to pale his uneffectual fire:
Adieu, adieu! Hamlet, remember me.

[Exit.]

HAMLET
O all you host of heaven! O earth! what else?
And shall I couple hell? O, fie!—Hold, my heart;
And you, my sinews, grow not instant old,
But bear me stiffly up.—Remember thee!
Ay, thou poor ghost, while memory holds a seat
In this distracted globe. Remember thee!
Yea, from the table of my memory
I'll wipe away all trivial fond records,
All saws of books, all forms, all pressures past,
That youth and observation copied there;
And thy commandment all alone shall live
Within the book and volume of my brain,
Unmix'd with baser matter: yes, by heaven!—
O most pernicious woman!
O villain, villain, smiling, damned villain!
My tables,—meet it is I set it down,
That one may smile, and smile, and be a villain;
At least, I am sure, it may be so in Denmark:

[Writing.]

So, uncle, there you are. Now to my word;
It is 'Adieu, adieu! remember me:'
I have sworn't.

HORATIO
[Within.] My lord, my lord,—

MARCELLUS
[Within.] Lord Hamlet,—

HORATIO
[Within.] Heaven secure him!

HAMLET
So be it!

MARCELLUS
[Within.] Illo, ho, ho, my lord!

HAMLET
Hillo, ho, ho, boy! Come, bird, come.

[Enter Horatio and Marcellus.]

MARCELLUS
How is't, my noble lord?

HORATIO
What news, my lord?

HAMLET
O, wonderful!

HORATIO
Good my lord, tell it.

HAMLET
No; you'll reveal it.

HORATIO
Not I, my lord, by heaven.

MARCELLUS
Nor I, my lord.

HAMLET
How say you then; would heart of man once think it?—
But you'll be secret?

HORATIO AND MARCELLUS
Ay, by heaven, my lord.

HAMLET
There's ne'er a villain dwelling in all Denmark
But he's an arrant knave.

HORATIO
There needs no ghost, my lord, come from the grave
To tell us this.

HAMLET
Why, right; you are i' the right;
And so, without more circumstance at all,
I hold it fit that we shake hands and part:
You, as your business and desires shall point you,—
For every man hath business and desire,
Such as it is;—and for my own poor part,
Look you, I'll go pray.

HORATIO
These are but wild and whirling words, my lord.

HAMLET
I'm sorry they offend you, heartily;
Yes, faith, heartily.

HORATIO
There's no offence, my lord.

HAMLET
Yes, by Saint Patrick, but there is, Horatio,
And much offence too. Touching this vision here,—
It is an honest ghost, that let me tell you:
For your desire to know what is between us,
O'ermaster't as you may. And now, good friends,
As you are friends, scholars, and soldiers,
Give me one poor request.

HORATIO
What is't, my lord? we will.

HAMLET
Never make known what you have seen to-night.

HORATIO AND MARCELLUS
My lord, we will not.

HAMLET
Nay, but swear't.

HORATIO
In faith,
My lord, not I.

MARCELLUS
Nor I, my lord, in faith.

HAMLET
Upon my sword.

MARCELLUS
We have sworn, my lord, already.

HAMLET
Indeed, upon my sword, indeed.

GHOST
[Beneath.] Swear.

HAMLET
Ha, ha boy! say'st thou so? art thou there, truepenny?—
Come on!—you hear this fellow in the cellarage,—
Consent to swear.

HORATIO
Propose the oath, my lord.

HAMLET
Never to speak of this that you have seen,
Swear by my sword.

GHOST
[Beneath.] Swear.

HAMLET
Hic et ubique? then we'll shift our ground.—
Come hither, gentlemen,
And lay your hands again upon my sword:
Never to speak of this that you have heard,
Swear by my sword.

GHOST
[Beneath.] Swear.

HAMLET
Well said, old mole! canst work i' the earth so fast?
A worthy pioner!—Once more remove, good friends.

HORATIO
O day and night, but this is wondrous strange!

HAMLET
And therefore as a stranger give it welcome.
There are more things in heaven and earth, Horatio,
Than are dreamt of in your philosophy.
But come;—
Here, as before, never, so help you mercy,
How strange or odd soe'er I bear myself,—
As I, perchance, hereafter shall think meet
To put an antic disposition on,—
That you, at such times seeing me, never shall,
With arms encumber'd thus, or this head-shake,
Or by pronouncing of some doubtful phrase,
As 'Well, well, we know'; or 'We could, an if we would';—
Or 'If we list to speak'; or 'There be, an if they might';—
Or such ambiguous giving out, to note
That you know aught of me:—this is not to do,
So grace and mercy at your most need help you,
Swear.

GHOST
[Beneath.] Swear.

HAMLET
Rest, rest, perturbed spirit!—So, gentlemen,
With all my love I do commend me to you:
And what so poor a man as Hamlet is
May do, to express his love and friending to you,
God willing, shall not lack. Let us go in together;
And still your fingers on your lips, I pray.

The time is out of joint:—O cursed spite,
That ever I was born to set it right!—
Nay, come, let's go together.

[Exeunt.]

ACT II

Scene I. A room in Polonius's house.

[Enter Polonius and Reynaldo.]

POLONIUS
Give him this money and these notes, Reynaldo.

REYNALDO
I will, my lord.

POLONIUS
You shall do marvellous wisely, good Reynaldo,
Before You visit him, to make inquiry
Of his behaviour.

REYNALDO
My lord, I did intend it.

POLONIUS
Marry, well said; very well said. Look you, sir,
Enquire me first what Danskers are in Paris;
And how, and who, what means, and where they keep,
What company, at what expense; and finding,
By this encompassment and drift of question,
That they do know my son, come you more nearer
Than your particular demands will touch it:
Take you, as 'twere, some distant knowledge of him;
As thus, 'I know his father and his friends,
And in part him;—do you mark this, Reynaldo?

REYNALDO
Ay, very well, my lord.

POLONIUS
'And in part him;—but,' you may say, 'not well:
But if't be he I mean, he's very wild;
Addicted so and so;' and there put on him
What forgeries you please; marry, none so rank
As may dishonour him; take heed of that;
But, sir, such wanton, wild, and usual slips
As are companions noted and most known
To youth and liberty.

REYNALDO
As gaming, my lord.

POLONIUS
Ay, or drinking, fencing, swearing, quarrelling,
Drabbing:—you may go so far.

REYNALDO
My lord, that would dishonour him.

POLONIUS
Faith, no; as you may season it in the charge.
You must not put another scandal on him,
That he is open to incontinency;
That's not my meaning: but breathe his faults so quaintly
That they may seem the taints of liberty;
The flash and outbreak of a fiery mind;
A savageness in unreclaimed blood,
Of general assault.

REYNALDO
But, my good lord,—

POLONIUS
Wherefore should you do this?

REYNALDO
Ay, my lord,
I would know that.

POLONIUS
Marry, sir, here's my drift;
And I believe it is a fetch of warrant:
You laying these slight sullies on my son
As 'twere a thing a little soil'd i' the working,
Mark you,
Your party in converse, him you would sound,
Having ever seen in the prenominate crimes
The youth you breathe of guilty, be assur'd
He closes with you in this consequence;
'Good sir,' or so; or 'friend,' or 'gentleman'—
According to the phrase or the addition
Of man and country.

REYNALDO
Very good, my lord.

POLONIUS
And then, sir, does he this,—he does—What was I about to say?—
By the mass, I was about to say something:—Where did I leave?

REYNALDO
At 'closes in the consequence,' at 'friend or so,' and gentleman.'

POLONIUS
At—closes in the consequence'—ay, marry!
He closes with you thus:—'I know the gentleman;
I saw him yesterday, or t'other day,
Or then, or then; with such, or such; and, as you say,
There was he gaming; there o'ertook in's rouse;
There falling out at tennis': or perchance,
'I saw him enter such a house of sale,'—
Videlicet, a brothel,—or so forth.—
See you now;
Your bait of falsehood takes this carp of truth:
And thus do we of wisdom and of reach,
With windlaces, and with assays of bias,
By indirections find directions out:

So, by my former lecture and advice,
Shall you my son. You have me, have you not?

REYNALDO
My lord, I have.

POLONIUS
God b' wi' you, fare you well.

REYNALDO
Good my lord!

POLONIUS
Observe his inclination in yourself.

REYNALDO
I shall, my lord.

POLONIUS
And let him ply his music.

REYNALDO
Well, my lord.

POLONIUS
Farewell!

[Exit Reynaldo.]

[Enter Ophelia.]

How now, Ophelia! what's the matter?

OPHELIA
Alas, my lord, I have been so affrighted!

POLONIUS
With what, i' the name of God?

OPHELIA
My lord, as I was sewing in my chamber,
Lord Hamlet,—with his doublet all unbrac'd;
No hat upon his head; his stockings foul'd,
Ungart'red, and down-gyved to his ankle;

Pale as his shirt; his knees knocking each other;
And with a look so piteous in purport
As if he had been loosed out of hell
To speak of horrors,—he comes before me.

POLONIUS
Mad for thy love?

OPHELIA
My lord, I do not know;
But truly I do fear it.

POLONIUS
What said he?

OPHELIA
He took me by the wrist, and held me hard;
Then goes he to the length of all his arm;
And with his other hand thus o'er his brow,
He falls to such perusal of my face
As he would draw it. Long stay'd he so;
At last,—a little shaking of mine arm,
And thrice his head thus waving up and down,—
He rais'd a sigh so piteous and profound
As it did seem to shatter all his bulk
And end his being: that done, he lets me go:
And, with his head over his shoulder turn'd
He seem'd to find his way without his eyes;
For out o' doors he went without their help,
And to the last bended their light on me.

POLONIUS
Come, go with me: I will go seek the king.
This is the very ecstasy of love;
Whose violent property fordoes itself,
And leads the will to desperate undertakings,
As oft as any passion under heaven
That does afflict our natures. I am sorry,—
What, have you given him any hard words of late?

OPHELIA
No, my good lord; but, as you did command,
I did repel his letters and denied
His access to me.

POLONIUS
That hath made him mad.
I am sorry that with better heed and judgment
I had not quoted him: I fear'd he did but trifle,
And meant to wreck thee; but beshrew my jealousy!
It seems it as proper to our age
To cast beyond ourselves in our opinions
As it is common for the younger sort
To lack discretion. Come, go we to the king:
This must be known; which, being kept close, might move
More grief to hide than hate to utter love.

[Exeunt.]

Scene II. A room in the Castle.

[Enter King, Rosencrantz, Guildenstern, and Attendants.]

KING
Welcome, dear Rosencrantz and Guildenstern!
Moreover that we much did long to see you,
The need we have to use you did provoke
Our hasty sending. Something have you heard
Of Hamlet's transformation; so I call it,
Since nor the exterior nor the inward man
Resembles that it was. What it should be,
More than his father's death, that thus hath put him
So much from the understanding of himself,
I cannot dream of: I entreat you both
That, being of so young days brought up with him,
And since so neighbour'd to his youth and humour,
That you vouchsafe your rest here in our court
Some little time: so by your companies
To draw him on to pleasures, and to gather,

So much as from occasion you may glean,
Whether aught, to us unknown, afflicts him thus,
That, open'd, lies within our remedy.

QUEEN
Good gentlemen, he hath much talk'd of you,
And sure I am two men there are not living
To whom he more adheres. If it will please you
To show us so much gentry and good-will
As to expend your time with us awhile,
For the supply and profit of our hope,
Your visitation shall receive such thanks
As fits a king's remembrance.

ROSENCRANTZ
Both your majesties
Might, by the sovereign power you have of us,
Put your dread pleasures more into command
Than to entreaty.

GUILDENSTERN
We both obey,
And here give up ourselves, in the full bent,
To lay our service freely at your feet,
To be commanded.

KING
Thanks, Rosencrantz and gentle Guildenstern.

QUEEN
Thanks, Guildenstern and gentle Rosencrantz:
And I beseech you instantly to visit
My too-much-changed son.—Go, some of you,
And bring these gentlemen where Hamlet is.

GUILDENSTERN
Heavens make our presence and our practices
Pleasant and helpful to him!

QUEEN
Ay, amen!

[Exeunt Rosencrantz, Guildenstern, and some Attendants.]

[Enter Polonius.]

POLONIUS
Th' ambassadors from Norway, my good lord,
Are joyfully return'd.

KING
Thou still hast been the father of good news.

POLONIUS
Have I, my lord? Assure you, my good liege,
I hold my duty, as I hold my soul,
Both to my God and to my gracious king:
And I do think,—or else this brain of mine
Hunts not the trail of policy so sure
As it hath us'd to do,—that I have found
The very cause of Hamlet's lunacy.

KING
O, speak of that; that do I long to hear.

POLONIUS
Give first admittance to the ambassadors;
My news shall be the fruit to that great feast.

KING
Thyself do grace to them, and bring them in.

[Exit Polonius.]

He tells me, my sweet queen, he hath found
The head and source of all your son's distemper.

QUEEN
I doubt it is no other but the main,—
His father's death and our o'erhasty marriage.

KING
Well, we shall sift him.

[Enter Polonius, with Voltimand and Cornelius.]

Welcome, my good friends!
Say, Voltimand, what from our brother Norway?

VOLTIMAND
Most fair return of greetings and desires.
Upon our first, he sent out to suppress
His nephew's levies; which to him appear'd
To be a preparation 'gainst the Polack;
But, better look'd into, he truly found
It was against your highness; whereat griev'd,—
That so his sickness, age, and impotence
Was falsely borne in hand,—sends out arrests
On Fortinbras; which he, in brief, obeys;
Receives rebuke from Norway; and, in fine,
Makes vow before his uncle never more
To give th' assay of arms against your majesty.
Whereon old Norway, overcome with joy,
Gives him three thousand crowns in annual fee;
And his commission to employ those soldiers,
So levied as before, against the Polack:
With an entreaty, herein further shown,
[Gives a paper.]
That it might please you to give quiet pass
Through your dominions for this enterprise,
On such regards of safety and allowance
As therein are set down.

KING
It likes us well;
And at our more consider'd time we'll read,
Answer, and think upon this business.
Meantime we thank you for your well-took labour:
Go to your rest; at night we'll feast together:
Most welcome home!

[Exeunt Voltimand and Cornelius.]

POLONIUS
This business is well ended.—

My liege, and madam,—to expostulate
What majesty should be, what duty is,
Why day is day, night is night, and time is time.
Were nothing but to waste night, day, and time.
Therefore, since brevity is the soul of wit,
And tediousness the limbs and outward flourishes,
I will be brief:—your noble son is mad:
Mad call I it; for to define true madness,
What is't but to be nothing else but mad?
But let that go.

QUEEN
More matter, with less art.

POLONIUS
Madam, I swear I use no art at all.
That he is mad, 'tis true: 'tis true 'tis pity;
And pity 'tis 'tis true: a foolish figure;
But farewell it, for I will use no art.
Mad let us grant him then: and now remains
That we find out the cause of this effect;
Or rather say, the cause of this defect,
For this effect defective comes by cause:
Thus it remains, and the remainder thus.
Perpend.
I have a daughter,—have whilst she is mine,—
Who, in her duty and obedience, mark,
Hath given me this: now gather, and surmise.
[Reads.]
    'To the celestial, and my soul's idol, the most beautified
Ophelia,'—
That's an ill phrase, a vile phrase; 'beautified' is a vile phrase: but
you shall hear. Thus:
[Reads.]
    'In her excellent white bosom, these, etc.'

QUEEN
Came this from Hamlet to her?

POLONIUS
Good madam, stay awhile; I will be faithful.
[Reads.]
   'Doubt thou the stars are fire;
      Doubt that the sun doth move;
   Doubt truth to be a liar;
      But never doubt I love.
   'O dear Ophelia, I am ill at these numbers; I have not art to
reckon my groans: but that I love thee best, O most best, believe
it. Adieu.
   'Thine evermore, most dear lady, whilst this machine is to him,
      HAMLET.'
This, in obedience, hath my daughter show'd me;
And more above, hath his solicitings,
As they fell out by time, by means, and place,
All given to mine ear.

KING
But how hath she
Receiv'd his love?

POLONIUS
What do you think of me?

KING
As of a man faithful and honourable.

POLONIUS
I would fain prove so. But what might you think,
When I had seen this hot love on the wing,—
As I perceiv'd it, I must tell you that,
Before my daughter told me,— what might you,
Or my dear majesty your queen here, think,
If I had play'd the desk or table-book,
Or given my heart a winking, mute and dumb;
Or look'd upon this love with idle sight;—
What might you think? No, I went round to work,
And my young mistress thus I did bespeak:

'Lord Hamlet is a prince, out of thy sphere;
This must not be:' and then I precepts gave her,
That she should lock herself from his resort,
Admit no messengers, receive no tokens.
Which done, she took the fruits of my advice;
And he, repulsed,—a short tale to make,—
Fell into a sadness; then into a fast;
Thence to a watch; thence into a weakness;
Thence to a lightness; and, by this declension,
Into the madness wherein now he raves,
And all we wail for.

KING
Do you think 'tis this?

QUEEN
It may be, very likely.

POLONIUS
Hath there been such a time,—I'd fain know that—
That I have positively said ''Tis so,'
When it prov'd otherwise?

KING
Not that I know.

POLONIUS
Take this from this, if this be otherwise:
[Points to his head and shoulder.]
If circumstances lead me, I will find
Where truth is hid, though it were hid indeed
Within the centre.

KING
How may we try it further?

POLONIUS
You know sometimes he walks for hours together
Here in the lobby.

QUEEN
So he does indeed.

POLONIUS
At such a time I'll loose my daughter to him:
Be you and I behind an arras then;
Mark the encounter: if he love her not,
And he not from his reason fall'n thereon
Let me be no assistant for a state,
But keep a farm and carters.

KING
We will try it.

QUEEN
But look where sadly the poor wretch comes reading.

POLONIUS
Away, I do beseech you, both away
I'll board him presently:—O, give me leave.

[Exeunt King, Queen, and Attendants.]

[Enter Hamlet, reading.]

How does my good Lord Hamlet?

HAMLET
Well, God-a-mercy.

POLONIUS
Do you know me, my lord?

HAMLET
Excellent well; you're a fishmonger.

POLONIUS
Not I, my lord.

HAMLET
Then I would you were so honest a man.

POLONIUS
Honest, my lord!

HAMLET
Ay, sir; to be honest, as this world goes, is to be one man picked
out of ten thousand.

POLONIUS
That's very true, my lord.

HAMLET
For if the sun breed maggots in a dead dog, being a god-kissing carrion,—Have you a daughter?

POLONIUS
I have, my lord.

HAMLET
Let her not walk i' the sun: conception is a blessing, but not as your daughter may conceive:—friend, look to't.

POLONIUS
How say you by that?—*[Aside.]* Still harping on my daughter:— yet he knew me not at first; he said I was a fishmonger: he is far gone, far gone: and truly in my youth I suffered much extremity for love; very near this. I'll speak to him again.—What do you read, my lord?

HAMLET
Words, words, words.

POLONIUS
What is the matter, my lord?

HAMLET
Between who?

POLONIUS
I mean, the matter that you read, my lord.

HAMLET
Slanders, sir: for the satirical slave says here that old men have grey beards; that their faces are wrinkled; their eyes purging thick amber and plum-tree gum; and that they have a plentiful lack of wit, together with most weak hams: all which, sir, though I most powerfully and potently believe, yet I hold it not honesty to have it thus set down; for you yourself, sir, should be old as I am, if, like a crab, you could go backward.

POLONIUS
[Aside.] Though this be madness, yet there is a method in't.—
Will you walk out of the air, my lord?

HAMLET
Into my grave?

POLONIUS
Indeed, that is out o' the air. *[Aside.]* How pregnant sometimes
his replies are! a happiness that often madness hits on, which reason and sanity could not so prosperously be delivered of. I will
leave him and suddenly contrive the means of meeting between
him and my daughter.—My honourable lord, I will most humbly
take my leave of you.

HAMLET
You cannot, sir, take from me anything that I will more willingly
part withal,—except my life, except my life, except my life.

POLONIUS
Fare you well, my lord.

HAMLET
These tedious old fools!

[Enter Rosencrantz and Guildenstern.]

POLONIUS
You go to seek the Lord Hamlet; there he is.

ROSENCRANTZ
[To Polonius.] God save you, sir!

[Exit Polonius.]

GUILDENSTERN
My honoured lord!

ROSENCRANTZ
My most dear lord!

HAMLET
My excellent good friends! How dost thou, Guildenstern? Ah,
Rosencrantz! Good lads, how do ye both?

ROSENCRANTZ
As the indifferent children of the earth.

GUILDENSTERN
Happy in that we are not over-happy;
On fortune's cap we are not the very button.

HAMLET
Nor the soles of her shoe?

ROSENCRANTZ
Neither, my lord.

HAMLET
Then you live about her waist, or in the middle of her favours?

GUILDENSTERN
Faith, her privates we.

HAMLET
In the secret parts of fortune? O, most true; she is a strumpet.
What's the news?

ROSENCRANTZ
None, my lord, but that the world's grown honest.

HAMLET
Then is doomsday near; but your news is not true. Let me question more in particular: what have you, my good friends, deserved at the hands of fortune, that she sends you to prison hither?

GUILDENSTERN
Prison, my lord!

HAMLET
Denmark's a prison.

ROSENCRANTZ
Then is the world one.

HAMLET
A goodly one; in which there are many confines, wards, and dungeons, Denmark being one o' the worst.

ROSENCRANTZ
We think not so, my lord.

HAMLET
Why, then 'tis none to you; for there is nothing either good or bad but thinking makes it so: to me it is a prison.

ROSENCRANTZ
Why, then, your ambition makes it one; 'tis too narrow for your mind.

HAMLET
O God, I could be bounded in a nutshell, and count myself a king of infinite space, were it not that I have bad dreams.

GUILDENSTERN
Which dreams, indeed, are ambition; for the very substance of the ambitious is merely the shadow of a dream.

HAMLET
A dream itself is but a shadow.

ROSENCRANTZ
Truly, and I hold ambition of so airy and light a quality that it is but a shadow's shadow.

HAMLET
Then are our beggars bodies, and our monarchs and outstretch'd heroes the beggars' shadows. Shall we to the court? for, by my fay, I cannot reason.

ROSENCRANTZ AND GUILDENSTERN
We'll wait upon you.

HAMLET
No such matter: I will not sort you with the rest of my servants; for, to speak to you like an honest man, I am most dreadfully attended. But, in the beaten way of friendship, what make you at Elsinore?

ROSENCRANTZ
To visit you, my lord; no other occasion.

HAMLET
Beggar that I am, I am even poor in thanks; but I thank you: and sure, dear friends, my thanks are too dear a halfpenny. Were you not sent for? Is it your own inclining? Is it a free visitation? Come, deal justly with me: come, come; nay, speak.

GUILDENSTERN
What should we say, my lord?

HAMLET
Why, anything—but to the purpose. You were sent for; and there is a kind of confession in your looks, which your modesties have not craft enough to colour: I know the good king and queen have sent for you.

ROSENCRANTZ
To what end, my lord?

HAMLET
That you must teach me. But let me conjure you, by the rights of our fellowship, by the consonancy of our youth, by the obligation of our ever-preserved love, and by what more dear a better proposer could charge you withal, be even and direct with me, whether you were sent for or no.

ROSENCRANTZ
[To Guildenstern.] What say you?

HAMLET
[Aside.] Nay, then, I have an eye of you.—If you love me, hold not off.

GUILDENSTERN
My lord, we were sent for.

HAMLET
I will tell you why; so shall my anticipation prevent your discovery, and your secrecy to the king and queen moult no feather. I have of late,—but wherefore I know not,—lost all my mirth, forgone all custom of exercises; and indeed, it goes so heavily with my disposition that this goodly frame, the earth, seems to me a

sterile promontory; this most excellent canopy, the air, look you, this brave o'erhanging firmament, this majestical roof fretted with golden fire,—why, it appears no other thing to me than a foul and pestilent congregation of vapours. What a piece of work is man! How noble in reason! how infinite in faculties! in form and moving, how express and admirable! in action how like an angel! in apprehension, how like a god! the beauty of the world! the paragon of animals! And yet, to me, what is this quintessence of dust? Man delights not me; no, nor woman neither, though by your smiling you seem to say so.

ROSENCRANTZ
My lord, there was no such stuff in my thoughts.

HAMLET
Why did you laugh then, when I said 'Man delights not me'?

ROSENCRANTZ
To think, my lord, if you delight not in man, what lenten entertainment the players shall receive from you: we coted them on the way; and hither are they coming to offer you service.

HAMLET
He that plays the king shall be welcome,—his majesty shall have tribute of me; the adventurous knight shall use his foil and target; the lover shall not sigh gratis; the humorous man shall end his part in peace; the clown shall make those laugh whose lungs are tickle o' the sere; and the lady shall say her mind freely, or the blank verse shall halt for't. What players are they?

ROSENCRANTZ
Even those you were wont to take such delight in,—the tragedians of the city.

HAMLET
How chances it they travel? their residence, both in reputation and profit, was better both ways.

ROSENCRANTZ
I think their inhibition comes by the means of the late innovation.

HAMLET
Do they hold the same estimation they did when I was in the city?
Are they so followed?

ROSENCRANTZ
No, indeed, are they not.

HAMLET
How comes it? do they grow rusty?

ROSENCRANTZ
Nay, their endeavour keeps in the wonted pace: but there is, sir, an
aery of children, little eyases, that cry out on the top of question,
and are most tyrannically clapped for't: these are now the fashion;
and so berattle the common stages,—so they call them,—that
many wearing rapiers are afraid of goose-quills and dare scarce
come thither.

HAMLET
What, are they children? who maintains 'em? How are they
escoted? Will they pursue the quality no longer than they can
sing? will they not say afterwards, if they should grow themselves to common players,—as it is most like, if their means are
no better,—their writers do them wrong to make them exclaim
against their own succession?

ROSENCRANTZ
Faith, there has been much to do on both sides; and the nation
holds it no sin to tarre them to controversy: there was, for awhile,
no money bid for argument unless the poet and the player went
to cuffs in the question.

HAMLET
Is't possible?

GUILDENSTERN
O, there has been much throwing about of brains.

HAMLET
Do the boys carry it away?

ROSENCRANTZ
Ay, that they do, my lord; Hercules and his load too.

HAMLET
It is not very strange; for my uncle is king of Denmark, and
those that would make mouths at him while my father lived, give
twenty, forty, fifty, a hundred ducats a-piece for his picture in
little. 'Sblood, there is something in this more than natural, if
philosophy could find it out.

[Flourish of trumpets within.]

GUILDENSTERN
There are the players.

HAMLET
Gentlemen, you are welcome to Elsinore. Your hands, come: the
appurtenance of welcome is fashion and ceremony: let me comply with you in this garb; lest my extent to the players, which I
tell you must show fairly outward, should more appear like entertainment than yours. You are welcome: but my uncle-father and
aunt-mother are deceived.

GUILDENSTERN
In what, my dear lord?

HAMLET
I am but mad north-north-west: when the wind is southerly I
know a hawk from a handsaw.

[Enter Polonius.]

POLONIUS
Well be with you, gentlemen!

HAMLET
Hark you, Guildenstern;—and you too;—at each ear a hearer:
that great baby you see there is not yet out of his swaddling
clouts.

ROSENCRANTZ
Happily he's the second time come to them; for they say an old
man is twice a child.

HAMLET
I will prophesy he comes to tell me of the players; mark it.——You
say right, sir: o' Monday morning; 'twas so indeed.

POLONIUS
My lord, I have news to tell you.

HAMLET
My lord, I have news to tell you. When Roscius was an actor in
Rome,——

POLONIUS
The actors are come hither, my lord.

HAMLET
Buzz, buzz!

POLONIUS
Upon my honour,——

HAMLET
Then came each actor on his ass,——

POLONIUS
The best actors in the world, either for tragedy, comedy, history,
pastoral, pastoral-comical, historical-pastoral, tragical-historical,
tragical-comical-historical-pastoral, scene individable, or poem
unlimited: Seneca cannot be too heavy nor Plautus too light. For
the law of writ and the liberty, these are the only men.

HAMLET
O Jephthah, judge of Israel, what a treasure hadst thou!

POLONIUS
What treasure had he, my lord?

HAMLET
Why——
    'One fair daughter, and no more,
    The which he loved passing well.'

POLONIUS
[Aside.] Still on my daughter.

HAMLET
Am I not i' the right, old Jephthah?

POLONIUS
If you call me Jephthah, my lord, I have a daughter that I love passing well.

HAMLET
Nay, that follows not.

POLONIUS
What follows, then, my lord?

HAMLET
Why— 'As by lot, God wot,' and then, you know, 'It came to pass, as most like it was—' The first row of the pious chanson will show you more; for look where my abridgment comes.

[Enter four or five Players.]

You are welcome, masters; welcome, all:—I am glad to see thee well.—welcome, good friends.—O, my old friend! Thy face is valanc'd since I saw thee last; comest thou to beard me in Denmark?—What, my young lady and mistress! By'r lady, your ladyship is nearer to heaven than when I saw you last, by the altitude of a chopine. Pray God, your voice, like a piece of uncurrent gold, be not cracked within the ring.—Masters, you are all welcome. We'll e'en to't like French falconers, fly at anything we see: we'll have a speech straight: come, give us a taste of your quality: come, a passionate speech.

1 PLAYER
What speech, my lord?

HAMLET
I heard thee speak me a speech once,—but it was never acted; or if it was, not above once; for the play, I remember, pleased not the million, 'twas caviare to the general; but it was,—as I received it, and others, whose judgments in such matters cried in the top of mine,—an excellent play, well digested in the scenes, set down with as much modesty as cunning. I remember, one said there were no sallets in the lines to make the matter savoury, nor no

matter in the phrase that might indite the author of affectation; but called it an honest method, as wholesome as sweet, and by very much more handsome than fine. One speech in it I chiefly loved: 'twas AEneas' tale to Dido, and thereabout of it especially where he speaks of Priam's slaughter: if it live in your memory, begin at this line;—let me see, let me see:—

> The rugged Pyrrhus, like th' Hyrcanian beast,—

it is not so:— it begins with Pyrrhus:—

> 'The rugged Pyrrhus,—he whose sable arms,
>   Black as his purpose, did the night resemble
>   When he lay couched in the ominous horse,—
>   Hath now this dread and black complexion smear'd
>   With heraldry more dismal; head to foot
>   Now is he total gules; horridly trick'd
>   With blood of fathers, mothers, daughters, sons,
>   Bak'd and impasted with the parching streets,
>   That lend a tyrannous and a damned light
>   To their vile murders: roasted in wrath and fire,
>   And thus o'ersized with coagulate gore,
>   With eyes like carbuncles, the hellish Pyrrhus
>   Old grandsire Priam seeks.'

So, proceed you.

Polonius
'Fore God, my lord, well spoken, with good accent and good discretion.

1 Player
>   Anon he finds him,
>   Striking too short at Greeks: his antique sword,
>   Rebellious to his arm, lies where it falls,
>   Repugnant to command: unequal match'd,
>   Pyrrhus at Priam drives; in rage strikes wide;
>   But with the whiff and wind of his fell sword
>   The unnerved father falls. Then senseless Ilium,

Seeming to feel this blow, with flaming top
Stoops to his base; and with a hideous crash
Takes prisoner Pyrrhus' ear: for lo! his sword,
Which was declining on the milky head
Of reverend Priam, seem'd i' the air to stick:
So, as a painted tyrant, Pyrrhus stood;
And, like a neutral to his will and matter,
Did nothing.
But as we often see, against some storm,
A silence in the heavens, the rack stand still,
The bold winds speechless, and the orb below
As hush as death, anon the dreadful thunder
Doth rend the region; so, after Pyrrhus' pause,
A roused vengeance sets him new a-work;
And never did the Cyclops' hammers fall
On Mars's armour, forg'd for proof eterne,
With less remorse than Pyrrhus' bleeding sword
Now falls on Priam.—
Out, out, thou strumpet, Fortune! All you gods,
In general synod, take away her power;
Break all the spokes and fellies from her wheel,
And bowl the round nave down the hill of heaven,
As low as to the fiends!

POLONIUS
This is too long.

HAMLET
It shall to the barber's, with your beard.—Pr'ythee say on.—
He's for a jig or a tale of bawdry, or he sleeps:—say on; come to
Hecuba.

1 PLAYER
    But who, O who, had seen the mobled queen,—

HAMLET
'The mobled queen'?

POLONIUS
That's good! 'Mobled queen' is good.

1 PLAYER

> Run barefoot up and down, threatening the flames
> With bisson rheum; a clout upon that head
> Where late the diadem stood, and for a robe,
> About her lank and all o'erteemed loins,
> A blanket, in the alarm of fear caught up;—
> Who this had seen, with tongue in venom steep'd,
> 'Gainst Fortune's state would treason have pronounc'd:
> But if the gods themselves did see her then,
> When she saw Pyrrhus make malicious sport
> In mincing with his sword her husband's limbs,
> The instant burst of clamour that she made,—
> Unless things mortal move them not at all,—
> Would have made milch the burning eyes of heaven,
> And passion in the gods.

POLONIUS

Look, whether he has not turn'd his colour, and has tears in's eyes.—Pray you, no more!

HAMLET

'Tis well. I'll have thee speak out the rest of this soon.— Good my lord, will you see the players well bestowed? Do you hear? Let them be well used; for they are the abstracts and brief chronicles of the time; after your death you were better have a bad epitaph than their ill report while you live.

POLONIUS

My lord, I will use them according to their desert.

HAMLET

Odd's bodikin, man, better: use every man after his desert, and who should scape whipping? Use them after your own honour and dignity: the less they deserve, the more merit is in your bounty. Take them in.

POLONIUS

Come, sirs.

HAMLET
Follow him, friends: we'll hear a play to-morrow.

[Exeunt Polonius with all the Players but the First.]

Dost thou hear me, old friend? Can you play 'The Murder of Gonzago'?

1 PLAYER
Ay, my lord.

HAMLET
We'll ha't to-morrow night. You could, for a need, study a speech of some dozen or sixteen lines which I would set down and insert in't? could you not?

1 PLAYER
Ay, my lord.

HAMLET
Very well.—Follow that lord; and look you mock him not.

[Exit First Player.]

—My good friends *[to Rosencrantz and Guild.]*, I'll leave you till night: you are welcome to Elsinore.

ROSENCRANTZ
Good my lord!

[Exeunt Rosencrantz and Guildenstern.]

HAMLET
Ay, so, God b' wi' ye!
Now I am alone.
O, what a rogue and peasant slave am I!
Is it not monstrous that this player here,
But in a fiction, in a dream of passion,
Could force his soul so to his own conceit
That from her working all his visage wan'd;
Tears in his eyes, distraction in's aspect,
A broken voice, and his whole function suiting

With forms to his conceit? And all for nothing!
For Hecuba?
What's Hecuba to him, or he to Hecuba,
That he should weep for her? What would he do,
Had he the motive and the cue for passion
That I have? He would drown the stage with tears
And cleave the general ear with horrid speech;
Make mad the guilty, and appal the free;
Confound the ignorant, and amaze, indeed,
The very faculties of eyes and ears.
Yet I,
A dull and muddy-mettled rascal, peak,
Like John-a-dreams, unpregnant of my cause,
And can say nothing; no, not for a king
Upon whose property and most dear life
A damn'd defeat was made. Am I a coward?
Who calls me villain? breaks my pate across?
Plucks off my beard and blows it in my face?
Tweaks me by the nose? gives me the lie i' the throat
As deep as to the lungs? who does me this, ha?
'Swounds, I should take it: for it cannot be
But I am pigeon-liver'd, and lack gall
To make oppression bitter; or ere this
I should have fatted all the region kites
With this slave's offal: bloody, bawdy villain!
Remorseless, treacherous, lecherous, kindless villain!
O, vengeance!
Why, what an ass am I! This is most brave,
That I, the son of a dear father murder'd,
Prompted to my revenge by heaven and hell,
Must, like a whore, unpack my heart with words
And fall a-cursing like a very drab,
A scullion!
Fie upon't! foh!—About, my brain! I have heard
That guilty creatures, sitting at a play,
Have by the very cunning of the scene

Been struck so to the soul that presently
They have proclaim'd their malefactions;
For murder, though it have no tongue, will speak
With most miraculous organ, I'll have these players
Play something like the murder of my father
Before mine uncle: I'll observe his looks;
I'll tent him to the quick: if he but blench,
I know my course. The spirit that I have seen
May be the devil: and the devil hath power
To assume a pleasing shape; yea, and perhaps
Out of my weakness and my melancholy,—
As he is very potent with such spirits,—
Abuses me to damn me: I'll have grounds
More relative than this.—the play's the thing
Wherein I'll catch the conscience of the king.

[Exit.]

ACT III

Scene I. A room in the Castle.

[Enter King, Queen, Polonius, Ophelia, Rosencrantz, and Guildenstern.]

KING
And can you, by no drift of circumstance,
Get from him why he puts on this confusion,
Grating so harshly all his days of quiet
With turbulent and dangerous lunacy?

ROSENCRANTZ
He does confess he feels himself distracted,
But from what cause he will by no means speak.

GUILDENSTERN
Nor do we find him forward to be sounded,
But, with a crafty madness, keeps aloof
When we would bring him on to some confession
Of his true state.

QUEEN
Did he receive you well?

ROSENCRANTZ
Most like a gentleman.

GUILDENSTERN
But with much forcing of his disposition.

ROSENCRANTZ
Niggard of question; but, of our demands,
Most free in his reply.

QUEEN
Did you assay him
To any pastime?

ROSENCRANTZ
Madam, it so fell out that certain players
We o'er-raught on the way: of these we told him,
And there did seem in him a kind of joy
To hear of it: they are about the court,
And, as I think, they have already order
This night to play before him.

POLONIUS
'Tis most true;
And he beseech'd me to entreat your majesties
To hear and see the matter.

KING
With all my heart; and it doth much content me
To hear him so inclin'd.—
Good gentlemen, give him a further edge,
And drive his purpose on to these delights.

ROSENCRANTZ
We shall, my lord.

[Exeunt Rosencrantz and Guildenstern.]

KING
Sweet Gertrude, leave us too;
For we have closely sent for Hamlet hither,

That he, as 'twere by accident, may here
Affront Ophelia:
Her father and myself,—lawful espials,—
Will so bestow ourselves that, seeing, unseen,
We may of their encounter frankly judge;
And gather by him, as he is behav'd,
If't be the affliction of his love or no
That thus he suffers for.

QUEEN
I shall obey you:—
And for your part, Ophelia, I do wish
That your good beauties be the happy cause
Of Hamlet's wildness: so shall I hope your virtues
Will bring him to his wonted way again,
To both your honours.

OPHELIA
Madam, I wish it may.

[Exit Queen Gertrude.]

POLONIUS
Ophelia, walk you here.—Gracious, so please you,
We will bestow ourselves.—*[To Ophelia.]* Read on this book;
That show of such an exercise may colour
Your loneliness.—We are oft to blame in this,—
'Tis too much prov'd,—that with devotion's visage
And pious action we do sugar o'er
The Devil himself.

KING
[Aside.] O, 'tis too true!
How smart a lash that speech doth give my conscience!
The harlot's cheek, beautied with plastering art,
Is not more ugly to the thing that helps it
Than is my deed to my most painted word:
O heavy burden!

POLONIUS
I hear him coming: let's withdraw, my lord.

[Exeunt King and Polonius.]

[Enter Hamlet.]

HAMLET
To be, or not to be,—that is the question:—
Whether 'tis nobler in the mind to suffer
The slings and arrows of outrageous fortune
Or to take arms against a sea of troubles,
And by opposing end them?—To die,—to sleep,—
No more; and by a sleep to say we end
The heartache, and the thousand natural shocks
That flesh is heir to,—'tis a consummation
Devoutly to be wish'd. To die,—to sleep;—
To sleep! perchance to dream:—ay, there's the rub;
For in that sleep of death what dreams may come,
When we have shuffled off this mortal coil,
Must give us pause: there's the respect
That makes calamity of so long life;
For who would bear the whips and scorns of time,
The oppressor's wrong, the proud man's contumely,
The pangs of despis'd love, the law's delay,
The insolence of office, and the spurns
That patient merit of the unworthy takes,
When he himself might his quietus make
With a bare bodkin? who would these fardels bear,
To grunt and sweat under a weary life,
But that the dread of something after death,—
The undiscover'd country, from whose bourn
No traveller returns,—puzzles the will,
And makes us rather bear those ills we have
Than fly to others that we know not of?
Thus conscience does make cowards of us all;
And thus the native hue of resolution
Is sicklied o'er with the pale cast of thought;

And enterprises of great pith and moment,
With this regard, their currents turn awry,
And lose the name of action.—Soft you now!
The fair Ophelia!—Nymph, in thy orisons
Be all my sins remember'd.

OPHELIA
Good my lord,
How does your honour for this many a day?

HAMLET
I humbly thank you; well, well, well.

OPHELIA
My lord, I have remembrances of yours
That I have longed long to re-deliver.
I pray you, now receive them.

HAMLET
No, not I;
I never gave you aught.

OPHELIA
My honour'd lord, you know right well you did;
And with them words of so sweet breath compos'd
As made the things more rich; their perfume lost,
Take these again; for to the noble mind
Rich gifts wax poor when givers prove unkind.
There, my lord.

HAMLET
Ha, ha! are you honest?

OPHELIA
My lord?

HAMLET
Are you fair?

OPHELIA
What means your lordship?

HAMLET

That if you be honest and fair, your honesty should admit no discourse to your beauty.

OPHELIA

Could beauty, my lord, have better commerce than with honesty?

HAMLET

Ay, truly; for the power of beauty will sooner transform honesty from what it is to a bawd than the force of honesty can translate beauty into his likeness: this was sometime a paradox, but now the time gives it proof. I did love you once.

OPHELIA

Indeed, my lord, you made me believe so.

HAMLET

You should not have believ'd me; for virtue cannot so inoculate our old stock but we shall relish of it: I loved you not.

OPHELIA

I was the more deceived.

HAMLET

Get thee to a nunnery: why wouldst thou be a breeder of sinners? I am myself indifferent honest; but yet I could accuse me of such things that it were better my mother had not borne me: I am very proud, revengeful, ambitious; with more offences at my beck than I have thoughts to put them in, imagination to give them shape, or time to act them in. What should such fellows as I do crawling between earth and heaven? We are arrant knaves, all; believe none of us. Go thy ways to a nunnery. Where's your father?

OPHELIA

At home, my lord.

HAMLET

Let the doors be shut upon him, that he may play the fool nowhere but in's own house. Farewell.

OPHELIA
O, help him, you sweet heavens!

HAMLET
If thou dost marry, I'll give thee this plague for thy dowry,—
be thou as chaste as ice, as pure as snow, thou shalt not escape
calumny. Get thee to a nunnery, go: farewell. Or, if thou wilt
needs marry, marry a fool; for wise men know well enough what
monsters you make of them. To a nunnery, go; and quickly too.
Farewell.

OPHELIA
O heavenly powers, restore him!

HAMLET
I have heard of your paintings too, well enough; God hath given
you one face, and you make yourselves another: you jig, you
amble, and you lisp, and nickname God's creatures, and make
your wantonness your ignorance. Go to, I'll no more on't; it hath
made me mad. I say, we will have no more marriages: those that
are married already, all but one, shall live; the rest shall keep as
they are. To a nunnery, go.

[Exit.]

OPHELIA
O, what a noble mind is here o'erthrown!
The courtier's, scholar's, soldier's, eye, tongue, sword,
The expectancy and rose of the fair state,
The glass of fashion and the mould of form,
The observ'd of all observers,—quite, quite down!
And I, of ladies most deject and wretched
That suck'd the honey of his music vows,
Now see that noble and most sovereign reason,
Like sweet bells jangled, out of tune and harsh;
That unmatch'd form and feature of blown youth
Blasted with ecstasy: O, woe is me,
To have seen what I have seen, see what I see!

[Re-enter King and Polonius.]

KING
Love! his affections do not that way tend;
Nor what he spake, though it lack'd form a little,
Was not like madness. There's something in his soul
O'er which his melancholy sits on brood;
And I do doubt the hatch and the disclose
Will be some danger: which for to prevent,
I have in quick determination
Thus set it down:—he shall with speed to England
For the demand of our neglected tribute:
Haply the seas, and countries different,
With variable objects, shall expel
This something-settled matter in his heart;
Whereon his brains still beating puts him thus
From fashion of himself. What think you on't?

POLONIUS
It shall do well: but yet do I believe
The origin and commencement of his grief
Sprung from neglected love.—How now, Ophelia!
You need not tell us what Lord Hamlet said;
We heard it all.—My lord, do as you please;
But if you hold it fit, after the play,
Let his queen mother all alone entreat him
To show his grief: let her be round with him;
And I'll be plac'd, so please you, in the ear
Of all their conference. If she find him not,
To England send him; or confine him where
Your wisdom best shall think.

KING
It shall be so:
Madness in great ones must not unwatch'd go.

[Exeunt.]

Scene II. A hall in the Castle.

[Enter Hamlet and certain Players.]

HAMLET

Speak the speech, I pray you, as I pronounced it to you, trippingly on the tongue: but if you mouth it, as many of your players do, I had as lief the town crier spoke my lines. Nor do not saw the air too much with your hand, thus, but use all gently: for in the very torrent, tempest, and, as I may say, whirlwind of passion, you must acquire and beget a temperance that may give it smoothness. O, it offends me to the soul, to hear a robustious periwig-pated fellow tear a passion to tatters, to very rags, to split the ears of the groundlings, who, for the most part, are capable of nothing but inexplicable dumb shows and noise: I would have such a fellow whipped for o'erdoing Termagant; it out-herods Herod: pray you avoid it.

I PLAYER

I warrant your honour.

HAMLET

Be not too tame neither; but let your own discretion be your tutor: suit the action to the word, the word to the action; with this special observance, that you o'erstep not the modesty of nature: for anything so overdone is from the purpose of playing, whose end, both at the first and now, was and is, to hold, as 'twere, the mirror up to nature; to show virtue her own image, scorn her own image, and the very age and body of the time his form and pressure. Now, this overdone, or come tardy off, though it make the unskilful laugh, cannot but make the judicious grieve; the censure of the which one must in your allowance, o'erweigh a whole theatre of others. O, there be players that I have seen play,—and heard others praise, and that highly,—not to speak it profanely, that, neither having the accent of Christians, nor the gait of Christian, pagan, nor man, have so strutted and bellowed that I have thought some of nature's journeymen had made men, and not made them well, they imitated humanity so abominably.

I PLAYER

I hope we have reform'd that indifferently with us, sir.

HAMLET
O, reform it altogether. And let those that play your clowns speak
no more than is set down for them: for there be of them that will
themselves laugh, to set on some quantity of barren spectators
to laugh too, though in the meantime some necessary question
of the play be then to be considered: that's villanous and shows
a most pitiful ambition in the fool that uses it. Go make you
ready.

[Exeunt Players.]

[Enter Polonius, Rosencrantz, and Guildenstern.]

How now, my lord! will the king hear this piece of work?

POLONIUS
And the queen too, and that presently.

HAMLET
Bid the players make haste.

[Exit Polonius.]

Will you two help to hasten them?

ROSENCRANTZ AND GUILDENSTERN
We will, my lord.

[Exeunt Rosencrantz and Guildenstern.]

HAMLET
What, ho, Horatio!

[Enter Horatio.]

HORATIO
Here, sweet lord, at your service.

HAMLET
Horatio, thou art e'en as just a man
As e'er my conversation cop'd withal.

HORATIO
O, my dear lord,—

HAMLET
Nay, do not think I flatter;
For what advancement may I hope from thee,
That no revenue hast, but thy good spirits,
To feed and clothe thee? Why should the poor be flatter'd?
No, let the candied tongue lick absurd pomp;
And crook the pregnant hinges of the knee
Where thrift may follow fawning. Dost thou hear?
Since my dear soul was mistress of her choice,
And could of men distinguish, her election
Hath seal'd thee for herself: for thou hast been
As one, in suffering all, that suffers nothing;
A man that Fortune's buffets and rewards
Hast ta'en with equal thanks: and bles'd are those
Whose blood and judgment are so well commingled
That they are not a pipe for Fortune's finger
To sound what stop she please. Give me that man
That is not passion's slave, and I will wear him
In my heart's core, ay, in my heart of heart,
As I do thee.—Something too much of this.—
There is a play to-night before the king;
One scene of it comes near the circumstance,
Which I have told thee, of my father's death:
I pr'ythee, when thou see'st that act a-foot,
Even with the very comment of thy soul
Observe mine uncle: if his occulted guilt
Do not itself unkennel in one speech,
It is a damned ghost that we have seen;
And my imaginations are as foul
As Vulcan's stithy. Give him heedful note;
For I mine eyes will rivet to his face;
And, after, we will both our judgments join
In censure of his seeming.

HORATIO
Well, my lord:
If he steal aught the whilst this play is playing,
And scape detecting, I will pay the theft.

HAMLET

They are coming to the play. I must be idle:
Get you a place.

[Danish march. A flourish. Enter King, Queen, Polonius, Ophelia, Rosencrantz, Guildenstern, and others.]

KING

How fares our cousin Hamlet?

HAMLET

Excellent, i' faith; of the chameleon's dish: I eat the air, promise-
crammed: you cannot feed capons so.

KING

I have nothing with this answer, Hamlet; these words are not
mine.

HAMLET

No, nor mine now. My lord, you play'd once i' the university, you
say? *[To Polonius.]*

POLONIUS

That did I, my lord, and was accounted a good actor.

HAMLET

What did you enact?

POLONIUS

I did enact Julius Caesar; I was kill'd i' the Capitol; Brutus killed
me.

HAMLET

It was a brute part of him to kill so capital a calf there.——Be the
players ready?

ROSENCRANTZ

Ay, my lord; they stay upon your patience.

QUEEN

Come hither, my dear Hamlet, sit by me.

HAMLET

No, good mother, here's metal more attractive.

POLONIUS
O, ho! do you mark that? *[To the King.]*

HAMLET
Lady, shall I lie in your lap?
[Lying down at Ophelia's feet.]

OPHELIA
No, my lord.

HAMLET
I mean, my head upon your lap?

OPHELIA
Ay, my lord.

HAMLET
Do you think I meant country matters?

OPHELIA
I think nothing, my lord.

HAMLET
That's a fair thought to lie between maids' legs.

OPHELIA
What is, my lord?

HAMLET
Nothing.

OPHELIA
You are merry, my lord.

HAMLET
Who, I?

OPHELIA
Ay, my lord.

HAMLET
O, your only jig-maker! What should a man do but be merry? for look you how cheerfully my mother looks, and my father died within's two hours.

OPHELIA
Nay, 'tis twice two months, my lord.

HAMLET
So long? Nay then, let the devil wear black, for I'll have a suit of
sables. O heavens! die two months ago, and not forgotten yet?
Then there's hope a great man's memory may outlive his life half
a year: but, by'r lady, he must build churches then; or else shall
he suffer not thinking on, with the hobby-horse, whose epitaph is
'For, O, for, O, the hobby-horse is forgot!'

[Trumpets sound. The dumb show enters.]

*[Enter a King and a Queen very lovingly; the Queen embracing him
and he her. She kneels, and makes show of protestation unto him. He
takes her up, and declines his head upon her neck: lays him down
upon a bank of flowers: she, seeing him asleep, leaves him. Anon
comes in a fellow, takes off his crown, kisses it, pours poison in the
king's ears, and exit. The Queen returns, finds the King dead, and
makes passionate action. The Poisoner with some three or four Mutes,
comes in again, seeming to lament with her. The dead body is carried
away. The Poisoner wooes the Queen with gifts; she seems loth and
unwilling awhile, but in the end accepts his love.]*

[Exeunt.]

OPHELIA
What means this, my lord?

HAMLET
Marry, this is miching mallecho; it means mischief.

OPHELIA
Belike this show imports the argument of the play.

[Enter Prologue.]

HAMLET
We shall know by this fellow: the players cannot keep counsel;
they'll tell all.

OPHELIA
Will he tell us what this show meant?

HAMLET
Ay, or any show that you'll show him: be not you ashamed to
show, he'll not shame to tell you what it means.

OPHELIA
You are naught, you are naught: I'll mark the play.

PROLOGUE
 For us, and for our tragedy,
 Here stooping to your clemency,
 We beg your hearing patiently.

HAMLET
Is this a prologue, or the posy of a ring?

OPHELIA
'Tis brief, my lord.

HAMLET
As woman's love.

[Enter a King and a Queen.]

PLAYER KING
Full thirty times hath Phoebus' cart gone round
Neptune's salt wash and Tellus' orbed ground,
And thirty dozen moons with borrow'd sheen
About the world have times twelve thirties been,
Since love our hearts, and Hymen did our hands,
Unite commutual in most sacred bands.

PLAYER QUEEN
So many journeys may the sun and moon
Make us again count o'er ere love be done!
But, woe is me, you are so sick of late,
So far from cheer and from your former state.
That I distrust you. Yet, though I distrust,
Discomfort you, my lord, it nothing must:
For women's fear and love holds quantity;
In neither aught, or in extremity.
Now, what my love is, proof hath made you know;
And as my love is siz'd, my fear is so:

Where love is great, the littlest doubts are fear;
Where little fears grow great, great love grows there.

PLAYER KING
Faith, I must leave thee, love, and shortly too;
My operant powers their functions leave to do:
And thou shalt live in this fair world behind,
Honour'd, belov'd, and haply one as kind
For husband shalt thou,—

PLAYER QUEEN
O, confound the rest!
Such love must needs be treason in my breast:
In second husband let me be accurst!
None wed the second but who kill'd the first.

HAMLET
[Aside.] Wormwood, wormwood!

PLAYER QUEEN
The instances that second marriage move
Are base respects of thrift, but none of love.
A second time I kill my husband dead
When second husband kisses me in bed.

PLAYER KING
I do believe you think what now you speak;
But what we do determine oft we break.
Purpose is but the slave to memory;
Of violent birth, but poor validity:
Which now, like fruit unripe, sticks on the tree;
But fall unshaken when they mellow be.
Most necessary 'tis that we forget
To pay ourselves what to ourselves is debt:
What to ourselves in passion we propose,
The passion ending, doth the purpose lose.
The violence of either grief or joy
Their own enactures with themselves destroy:
Where joy most revels, grief doth most lament;

HAMLET

Grief joys, joy grieves, on slender accident.
This world is not for aye; nor 'tis not strange
That even our loves should with our fortunes change;
For 'tis a question left us yet to prove,
Whether love lead fortune, or else fortune love.
The great man down, you mark his favourite flies,
The poor advanc'd makes friends of enemies;
And hitherto doth love on fortune tend:
For who not needs shall never lack a friend;
And who in want a hollow friend doth try,
Directly seasons him his enemy.
But, orderly to end where I begun,—
Our wills and fates do so contrary run
That our devices still are overthrown;
Our thoughts are ours, their ends none of our own:
So think thou wilt no second husband wed;
But die thy thoughts when thy first lord is dead.

PLAYER QUEEN
Nor earth to me give food, nor heaven light!
Sport and repose lock from me day and night!
To desperation turn my trust and hope!
An anchor's cheer in prison be my scope!
Each opposite that blanks the face of joy
Meet what I would have well, and it destroy!
Both here and hence pursue me lasting strife,
If, once a widow, ever I be wife!

HAMLET
If she should break it now! *[To Ophelia.]*

PLAYER KING
'Tis deeply sworn. Sweet, leave me here awhile;
My spirits grow dull, and fain I would beguile
The tedious day with sleep.
[Sleeps.]

PLAYER QUEEN
Sleep rock thy brain,
And never come mischance between us twain!

[Exit.]

HAMLET
Madam, how like you this play?

QUEEN
The lady protests too much, methinks.

HAMLET
O, but she'll keep her word.

KING
Have you heard the argument? Is there no offence in't?

HAMLET
No, no! They do but jest, poison in jest; no offence i' the world.

KING
What do you call the play?
HAMLET
The Mouse-trap. Marry, how? Tropically. This play is the image of a murder done in Vienna: Gonzago is the duke's name; his wife, Baptista: you shall see anon; 'tis a knavish piece of work: but what o' that? your majesty, and we that have free souls, it touches us not: let the gall'd jade wince; our withers are unwrung.

[Enter Lucianus.]

This is one Lucianus, nephew to the King.

OPHELIA
You are a good chorus, my lord.

HAMLET
I could interpret between you and your love, if I could see the puppets dallying.

OPHELIA
You are keen, my lord, you are keen.

HAMLET
It would cost you a groaning to take off my edge.

OPHELIA
Still better, and worse.

HAMLET
So you must take your husbands.—Begin, murderer; pox, leave thy damnable faces, and begin. Come:—'The croaking raven doth bellow for revenge.'

LUCIANUS
Thoughts black, hands apt, drugs fit, and time agreeing;
Confederate season, else no creature seeing;
Thou mixture rank, of midnight weeds collected,
With Hecate's ban thrice blasted, thrice infected,
Thy natural magic and dire property
On wholesome life usurp immediately.

[Pours the poison into the sleeper's ears.]

HAMLET
He poisons him i' the garden for's estate. His name's Gonzago: The story is extant, and written in very choice Italian; you shall see anon how the murderer gets the love of Gonzago's wife.

OPHELIA
The King rises.

HAMLET
What, frighted with false fire!

QUEEN
How fares my lord?

POLONIUS
Give o'er the play.

KING
Give me some light:—away!

ALL
Lights, lights, lights!

[Exeunt all but Hamlet and Horatio.]

HAMLET

> Why, let the strucken deer go weep,
>> The hart ungalled play;
> For some must watch, while some must sleep:
>> So runs the world away.—

Would not this, sir, and a forest of feathers—if the rest of my fortunes turn Turk with me,—with two Provincial roses on my razed shoes, get me a fellowship in a cry of players, sir?

HORATIO

Half a share.

HAMLET

> A whole one, I.
> For thou dost know, O Damon dear,
>> This realm dismantled was
> Of Jove himself; and now reigns here
>> A very, very—pajock.

HORATIO

You might have rhymed.

HAMLET

O good Horatio, I'll take the ghost's word for a thousand pound! Didst perceive?

HORATIO

Very well, my lord.

HAMLET

Upon the talk of the poisoning?—

HORATIO

I did very well note him.

HAMLET

Ah, ha!—Come, some music! Come, the recorders!—

> For if the king like not the comedy,
>> Why then, belike he likes it not, perdy.

Come, some music!

[Enter Rosencrantz and Guildenstern.]

GUILDENSTERN
Good my lord, vouchsafe me a word with you.

HAMLET
Sir, a whole history.

GUILDENSTERN
The king, sir—

HAMLET
Ay, sir, what of him?

GUILDENSTERN
Is, in his retirement, marvellous distempered.

HAMLET
With drink, sir?

GUILDENSTERN
No, my lord; rather with choler.

HAMLET
Your wisdom should show itself more richer to signify this to the doctor; for me to put him to his purgation would perhaps plunge him into far more choler.

GUILDENSTERN
Good my lord, put your discourse into some frame, and start not so wildly from my affair.

HAMLET
I am tame, sir:—pronounce.

GUILDENSTERN
The queen, your mother, in most great affliction of spirit, hath sent me to you.

HAMLET
You are welcome.

GUILDENSTERN
Nay, good my lord, this courtesy is not of the right breed. If it shall please you to make me a wholesome answer, I will do your

mother's commandment: if not, your pardon and my return shall be the end of my business.

HAMLET
Sir, I cannot.

GUILDENSTERN
What, my lord?

HAMLET
Make you a wholesome answer; my wit's diseased: but, sir, such answer as I can make, you shall command; or rather, as you say, my mother: therefore no more, but to the matter: my mother, you say,—

ROSENCRANTZ
Then thus she says: your behaviour hath struck her into amazement and admiration.

HAMLET
O wonderful son, that can so stonish a mother!—But is there no sequel at the heels of this mother's admiration?

ROSENCRANTZ
She desires to speak with you in her closet ere you go to bed.

HAMLET
We shall obey, were she ten times our mother. Have you any further trade with us?

ROSENCRANTZ
My lord, you once did love me.

HAMLET
And so I do still, by these pickers and stealers.

ROSENCRANTZ
Good my lord, what is your cause of distemper? you do, surely, bar the door upon your own liberty if you deny your griefs to your friend.

HAMLET
Sir, I lack advancement.

ROSENCRANTZ
How can that be, when you have the voice of the king himself for
your succession in Denmark?

HAMLET
Ay, sir, but 'While the grass grows'—the proverb is something
musty.

[Re-enter the Players, with recorders.]

O, the recorders:—let me see one.—To withdraw with you:—
why do you go about to recover the wind of me, as if you would
drive me into a toil?

GUILDENSTERN
O my lord, if my duty be too bold, my love is too unmannerly.

HAMLET
I do not well understand that. Will you play upon this pipe?

GUILDENSTERN
My lord, I cannot.

HAMLET
I pray you.

GUILDENSTERN
Believe me, I cannot.

HAMLET
I do beseech you.

GUILDENSTERN
I know, no touch of it, my lord.

HAMLET
'Tis as easy as lying: govern these ventages with your finger and
thumb, give it breath with your mouth, and it will discourse most
eloquent music. Look you, these are the stops.

GUILDENSTERN
But these cannot I command to any utterance of harmony; I have
not the skill.

HAMLET
Why, look you now, how unworthy a thing you make of me! You would play upon me; you would seem to know my stops; you would pluck out the heart of my mystery; you would sound me from my lowest note to the top of my compass; and there is much music, excellent voice, in this little organ, yet cannot you make it speak. 'Sblood, do you think I am easier to be played on than a pipe? Call me what instrument you will, though you can fret me, you cannot play upon me.

[Enter Polonius.]

God bless you, sir!

POLONIUS
My lord, the queen would speak with you, and presently.
HAMLET
Do you see yonder cloud that's almost in shape of a camel?

POLONIUS
By the mass, and 'tis like a camel indeed.

HAMLET
Methinks it is like a weasel.

POLONIUS
It is backed like a weasel.

HAMLET
Or like a whale.

POLONIUS
Very like a whale.

HAMLET
Then will I come to my mother by and by.—*[Aside.]* They fool me to the top of my bent.—I will come by and by.

POLONIUS
I will say so.

[Exit.]

HAMLET
By-and-by is easily said.

[Exit Polonius.]

—Leave me, friends.

[Exeunt Rosencrantz, Guildenstern, Horatio, and Players.]

'Tis now the very witching time of night,
When churchyards yawn, and hell itself breathes out
Contagion to this world: now could I drink hot blood,
And do such bitter business as the day
Would quake to look on. Soft! now to my mother.—
O heart, lose not thy nature; let not ever
The soul of Nero enter this firm bosom:
Let me be cruel, not unnatural;
I will speak daggers to her, but use none;
My tongue and soul in this be hypocrites,—
How in my words somever she be shent,
To give them seals never, my soul, consent!

[Exit.]

Scene III. A room in the Castle.

[Enter King, Rosencrantz, and Guildenstern.]

KING
I like him not; nor stands it safe with us
To let his madness range. Therefore prepare you;
I your commission will forthwith dispatch,
And he to England shall along with you:
The terms of our estate may not endure
Hazard so near us as doth hourly grow
Out of his lunacies.

GUILDENSTERN
We will ourselves provide:
Most holy and religious fear it is
To keep those many many bodies safe
That live and feed upon your majesty.

ROSENCRANTZ
The single and peculiar life is bound,
With all the strength and armour of the mind,
To keep itself from 'noyance; but much more
That spirit upon whose weal depend and rest
The lives of many. The cease of majesty
Dies not alone; but like a gulf doth draw
What's near it with it: it is a massy wheel,
Fix'd on the summit of the highest mount,
To whose huge spokes ten thousand lesser things
Are mortis'd and adjoin'd; which, when it falls,
Each small annexment, petty consequence,
Attends the boisterous ruin. Never alone
Did the king sigh, but with a general groan.

KING
Arm you, I pray you, to this speedy voyage;
For we will fetters put upon this fear,
Which now goes too free-footed.

ROSENCRANTZ AND GUILDENSTERN
We will haste us.

[Exeunt Rosencrantz and Guildenstern.]

[Enter Polonius.]

POLONIUS
My lord, he's going to his mother's closet:
Behind the arras I'll convey myself
To hear the process; I'll warrant she'll tax him home:
And, as you said, and wisely was it said,
'Tis meet that some more audience than a mother,
Since nature makes them partial, should o'erhear
The speech, of vantage. Fare you well, my liege:
I'll call upon you ere you go to bed,
And tell you what I know.

KING
Thanks, dear my lord.

[Exit Polonius.]

O, my offence is rank, it smells to heaven;
It hath the primal eldest curse upon't,—
A brother's murder!—Pray can I not,
Though inclination be as sharp as will:
My stronger guilt defeats my strong intent;
And, like a man to double business bound,
I stand in pause where I shall first begin,
And both neglect. What if this cursed hand
Were thicker than itself with brother's blood,—
Is there not rain enough in the sweet heavens
To wash it white as snow? Whereto serves mercy
But to confront the visage of offence?
And what's in prayer but this twofold force,—
To be forestalled ere we come to fall,
Or pardon'd being down? Then I'll look up;
My fault is past. But, O, what form of prayer
Can serve my turn? Forgive me my foul murder!—
That cannot be; since I am still possess'd
Of those effects for which I did the murder,—
My crown, mine own ambition, and my queen.
May one be pardon'd and retain the offence?
In the corrupted currents of this world
Offence's gilded hand may shove by justice;
And oft 'tis seen the wicked prize itself
Buys out the law; but 'tis not so above;
There is no shuffling;—there the action lies
In his true nature; and we ourselves compell'd,
Even to the teeth and forehead of our faults,
To give in evidence. What then? what rests?
Try what repentance can: what can it not?
Yet what can it when one cannot repent?
O wretched state! O bosom black as death!
O limed soul, that, struggling to be free,
Art more engag'd! Help, angels! Make assay:
Bow, stubborn knees; and, heart, with strings of steel,

Be soft as sinews of the new-born babe!
All may be well.

[Retires and kneels.]

[Enter Hamlet.]

HAMLET
Now might I do it pat, now he is praying;
And now I'll do't;—and so he goes to heaven;
And so am I reveng'd.—that would be scann'd:
A villain kills my father; and for that,
I, his sole son, do this same villain send
To heaven.
O, this is hire and salary, not revenge.
He took my father grossly, full of bread;
With all his crimes broad blown, as flush as May;
And how his audit stands, who knows save heaven?
But in our circumstance and course of thought,
'Tis heavy with him: and am I, then, reveng'd,
To take him in the purging of his soul,
When he is fit and season'd for his passage?
No.
Up, sword, and know thou a more horrid hent:
When he is drunk asleep; or in his rage;
Or in the incestuous pleasure of his bed;
At gaming, swearing; or about some act
That has no relish of salvation in't;—
Then trip him, that his heels may kick at heaven;
And that his soul may be as damn'd and black
As hell, whereto it goes. My mother stays:
This physic but prolongs thy sickly days.

[Exit.]

[The King rises and advances.]

KING
My words fly up, my thoughts remain below:
Words without thoughts never to heaven go.

[Exit.]

Scene IV. Another room in the castle.

[Enter Queen and Polonius.]

POLONIUS
He will come straight. Look you lay home to him:
Tell him his pranks have been too broad to bear with,
And that your grace hath screen'd and stood between
Much heat and him. I'll silence me e'en here.
Pray you, be round with him.

HAMLET
[Within.] Mother, mother, mother!
QUEEN
I'll warrant you:
Fear me not:—withdraw; I hear him coming.

[Polonius goes behind the arras.]

[Enter Hamlet.]

HAMLET
Now, mother, what's the matter?

QUEEN
Hamlet, thou hast thy father much offended.

HAMLET
Mother, you have my father much offended.

QUEEN
Come, come, you answer with an idle tongue.

HAMLET
Go, go, you question with a wicked tongue.

QUEEN
Why, how now, Hamlet!

HAMLET
What's the matter now?

QUEEN
Have you forgot me?

HAMLET
No, by the rood, not so:
You are the queen, your husband's brother's wife,
And,—would it were not so!—you are my mother.

QUEEN
Nay, then, I'll set those to you that can speak.

HAMLET
Come, come, and sit you down; you shall not budge;
You go not till I set you up a glass
Where you may see the inmost part of you.

QUEEN
What wilt thou do? thou wilt not murder me?—
Help, help, ho!

POLONIUS
[Behind.] What, ho! help, help, help!

HAMLET
How now? a rat? *[Draws.]*
Dead for a ducat, dead!

[Makes a pass through the arras.]

POLONIUS
[Behind.] O, I am slain!

[Falls and dies.]

QUEEN
O me, what hast thou done?

HAMLET
Nay, I know not: is it the king?

[Draws forth Polonius.]

QUEEN
O, what a rash and bloody deed is this!

HAMLET
A bloody deed!—almost as bad, good mother,
As kill a king and marry with his brother.

QUEEN
As kill a king!

HAMLET
Ay, lady, 'twas my word.—
Thou wretched, rash, intruding fool, farewell!
[To Polonius.]
I took thee for thy better: take thy fortune;
Thou find'st to be too busy is some danger.—
Leave wringing of your hands: peace! sit you down,
And let me wring your heart: for so I shall,
If it be made of penetrable stuff;
If damned custom have not braz'd it so
That it is proof and bulwark against sense.

QUEEN
What have I done, that thou dar'st wag thy tongue
In noise so rude against me?

HAMLET
Such an act
That blurs the grace and blush of modesty;
Calls virtue hypocrite; takes off the rose
From the fair forehead of an innocent love,
And sets a blister there; makes marriage-vows
As false as dicers' oaths: O, such a deed
As from the body of contraction plucks
The very soul, and sweet religion makes
A rhapsody of words: heaven's face doth glow;
Yea, this solidity and compound mass,
With tristful visage, as against the doom,
Is thought-sick at the act.

QUEEN
Ah me, what act,
That roars so loud, and thunders in the index?

HAMLET
Look here upon this picture, and on this,—
The counterfeit presentment of two brothers.
See what a grace was seated on this brow;
Hyperion's curls; the front of Jove himself;
An eye like Mars, to threaten and command;
A station like the herald Mercury
New lighted on a heaven-kissing hill:
A combination and a form, indeed,
Where every god did seem to set his seal,
To give the world assurance of a man;
This was your husband.—Look you now what follows:
Here is your husband, like a milldew'd ear
Blasting his wholesome brother. Have you eyes?
Could you on this fair mountain leave to feed,
And batten on this moor? Ha! have you eyes?
You cannot call it love; for at your age
The hey-day in the blood is tame, it's humble,
And waits upon the judgment: and what judgment
Would step from this to this? Sense, sure, you have,
Else could you not have motion: but sure that sense
Is apoplex'd; for madness would not err;
Nor sense to ecstacy was ne'er so thrall'd
But it reserv'd some quantity of choice
To serve in such a difference. What devil was't
That thus hath cozen'd you at hoodman-blind?
Eyes without feeling, feeling without sight,
Ears without hands or eyes, smelling sans all,
Or but a sickly part of one true sense
Could not so mope.
O shame! where is thy blush? Rebellious hell,
If thou canst mutine in a matron's bones,
To flaming youth let virtue be as wax,
And melt in her own fire: proclaim no shame
When the compulsive ardour gives the charge,
Since frost itself as actively doth burn,
And reason panders will.

QUEEN
O Hamlet, speak no more:
Thou turn'st mine eyes into my very soul;
And there I see such black and grained spots
As will not leave their tinct.

HAMLET
Nay, but to live
In the rank sweat of an enseamed bed,
Stew'd in corruption, honeying and making love
Over the nasty sty,—

QUEEN
O, speak to me no more;
These words like daggers enter in mine ears;
No more, sweet Hamlet.

HAMLET
A murderer and a villain;
A slave that is not twentieth part the tithe
Of your precedent lord; a vice of kings;
A cutpurse of the empire and the rule,
That from a shelf the precious diadem stole
And put it in his pocket!

QUEEN
No more.

HAMLET
A king of shreds and patches!—

[Enter Ghost.]

Save me and hover o'er me with your wings,
You heavenly guards!—What would your gracious figure?

QUEEN
Alas, he's mad!

HAMLET
Do you not come your tardy son to chide,
That, laps'd in time and passion, lets go by

The important acting of your dread command?
O, say!

GHOST
Do not forget. This visitation
Is but to whet thy almost blunted purpose.
But, look, amazement on thy mother sits:
O, step between her and her fighting soul,—
Conceit in weakest bodies strongest works,—
Speak to her, Hamlet.

HAMLET
How is it with you, lady?

QUEEN
Alas, how is't with you,
That you do bend your eye on vacancy,
And with the incorporal air do hold discourse?
Forth at your eyes your spirits wildly peep;
And, as the sleeping soldiers in the alarm,
Your bedded hairs, like life in excrements,
Start up and stand an end. O gentle son,
Upon the heat and flame of thy distemper
Sprinkle cool patience! Whereon do you look?

HAMLET
On him, on him! Look you how pale he glares!
His form and cause conjoin'd, preaching to stones,
Would make them capable.—Do not look upon me;
Lest with this piteous action you convert
My stern effects: then what I have to do
Will want true colour; tears perchance for blood.

QUEEN
To whom do you speak this?

HAMLET
Do you see nothing there?

QUEEN
Nothing at all; yet all that is I see.

HAMLET
Nor did you nothing hear?

QUEEN
No, nothing but ourselves.

HAMLET
Why, look you there! look how it steals away!
My father, in his habit as he liv'd!
Look, where he goes, even now out at the portal!
[Exit Ghost.]

QUEEN
This is the very coinage of your brain:
This bodiless creation ecstasy
Is very cunning in.

HAMLET
Ecstasy!
My pulse, as yours, doth temperately keep time,
And makes as healthful music: it is not madness
That I have utter'd: bring me to the test,
And I the matter will re-word; which madness
Would gambol from. Mother, for love of grace,
Lay not that flattering unction to your soul
That not your trespass, but my madness speaks:
It will but skin and film the ulcerous place,
Whilst rank corruption, mining all within,
Infects unseen. Confess yourself to heaven;
Repent what's past; avoid what is to come;
And do not spread the compost on the weeds,
To make them ranker. Forgive me this my virtue;
For in the fatness of these pursy times
Virtue itself of vice must pardon beg,
Yea, curb and woo for leave to do him good.

QUEEN
O Hamlet, thou hast cleft my heart in twain.

HAMLET
O, throw away the worser part of it,
And live the purer with the other half.
Good night: but go not to mine uncle's bed;
Assume a virtue, if you have it not.
That monster custom, who all sense doth eat,
Of habits evil, is angel yet in this,—
That to the use of actions fair and good
He likewise gives a frock or livery
That aptly is put on. Refrain to-night;
And that shall lend a kind of easiness
To the next abstinence: the next more easy;
For use almost can change the stamp of nature,
And either curb the devil, or throw him out
With wondrous potency. Once more, good-night:
And when you are desirous to be bles'd,
I'll blessing beg of you.—For this same lord
[Pointing to Polonius.]
I do repent; but heaven hath pleas'd it so,
To punish me with this, and this with me,
That I must be their scourge and minister.
I will bestow him, and will answer well
The death I gave him. So again, good-night.—
I must be cruel, only to be kind:
Thus bad begins, and worse remains behind.—
One word more, good lady.

QUEEN
What shall I do?

HAMLET
Not this, by no means, that I bid you do:
Let the bloat king tempt you again to bed;
Pinch wanton on your cheek; call you his mouse;
And let him, for a pair of reechy kisses,
Or paddling in your neck with his damn'd fingers,
Make you to ravel all this matter out,

That I essentially am not in madness,
But mad in craft. 'Twere good you let him know;
For who that's but a queen, fair, sober, wise,
Would from a paddock, from a bat, a gib,
Such dear concernings hide? who would do so?
No, in despite of sense and secrecy,
Unpeg the basket on the house's top,
Let the birds fly, and, like the famous ape,
To try conclusions, in the basket creep
And break your own neck down.

QUEEN
Be thou assur'd, if words be made of breath,
And breath of life, I have no life to breathe
What thou hast said to me.

HAMLET
I must to England; you know that?

QUEEN
Alack,
I had forgot: 'tis so concluded on.

HAMLET
There's letters seal'd: and my two schoolfellows,—
Whom I will trust as I will adders fang'd,—
They bear the mandate; they must sweep my way
And marshal me to knavery. Let it work;
For 'tis the sport to have the enginer
Hoist with his own petard: and 't shall go hard
But I will delve one yard below their mines
And blow them at the moon: O, 'tis most sweet,
When in one line two crafts directly meet.—
This man shall set me packing:
I'll lug the guts into the neighbour room.—
Mother, good-night.—Indeed, this counsellor
Is now most still, most secret, and most grave,
Who was in life a foolish peating knave.

Come, sir, to draw toward an end with you:—
Good night, mother.

[Exeunt severally; Hamlet, dragging out Polonius.]

ACT IV

Scene I. A room in the Castle.

[Enter King, Queen, Rosencrantz and Guildenstern.]

KING
There's matter in these sighs. These profound heaves
You must translate: 'tis fit we understand them.
Where is your son?

QUEEN
Bestow this place on us a little while.

[To Rosencrantz and Guildenstern, who go out.]

Ah, my good lord, what have I seen to-night!

KING
What, Gertrude? How does Hamlet?

QUEEN
Mad as the sea and wind, when both contend
Which is the mightier: in his lawless fit
Behind the arras hearing something stir,
Whips out his rapier, cries 'A rat, a rat!'
And in this brainish apprehension, kills
The unseen good old man.

KING
O heavy deed!
It had been so with us, had we been there:
His liberty is full of threats to all;
To you yourself, to us, to every one.
Alas, how shall this bloody deed be answer'd?
It will be laid to us, whose providence
Should have kept short, restrain'd, and out of haunt
This mad young man. But so much was our love

We would not understand what was most fit;
But, like the owner of a foul disease,
To keep it from divulging, let it feed
Even on the pith of life. Where is he gone?

QUEEN
To draw apart the body he hath kill'd:
O'er whom his very madness, like some ore
Among a mineral of metals base,
Shows itself pure: he weeps for what is done.

KING
O Gertrude, come away!
The sun no sooner shall the mountains touch
But we will ship him hence: and this vile deed
We must with all our majesty and skill
Both countenance and excuse.—Ho, Guildenstern!

[Re-enter Rosencrantz and Guildenstern.]

Friends both, go join you with some further aid:
Hamlet in madness hath Polonius slain,
And from his mother's closet hath he dragg'd him:
Go seek him out; speak fair, and bring the body
Into the chapel. I pray you, haste in this.

[Exeunt Rosencrantz and Guildenstern.]

Come, Gertrude, we'll call up our wisest friends;
And let them know both what we mean to do
And what's untimely done: so haply slander,—
Whose whisper o'er the world's diameter,
As level as the cannon to his blank,
Transports his poison'd shot,—may miss our name,
And hit the woundless air.—O, come away!
My soul is full of discord and dismay.

[Exeunt.]

Scene II. Another room in the Castle.

[Enter Hamlet.]

HAMLET
Safely stowed.

ROSENCRANTZ AND GUILDENSTERN
[Within.] Hamlet! Lord Hamlet!

HAMLET
What noise? who calls on Hamlet? O, here they come.

[Enter Rosencrantz and Guildenstern.]

ROSENCRANTZ
What have you done, my lord, with the dead body?

HAMLET
Compounded it with dust, whereto 'tis kin.

ROSENCRANTZ
Tell us where 'tis, that we may take it thence,
And bear it to the chapel.

HAMLET
Do not believe it.

ROSENCRANTZ
Believe what?

HAMLET
That I can keep your counsel, and not mine own. Besides, to be
demanded of a sponge!—what replication should be made by the
son of a king?

ROSENCRANTZ
Take you me for a sponge, my lord?

HAMLET
Ay, sir; that soaks up the King's countenance, his rewards, his
authorities. But such officers do the king best service in the end:
he keeps them, like an ape, in the corner of his jaw; first mouthed,

to be last swallowed: when he needs what you have gleaned, it is but squeezing you, and, sponge, you shall be dry again.

ROSENCRANTZ
I understand you not, my lord.

HAMLET
I am glad of it: a knavish speech sleeps in a foolish ear.

ROSENCRANTZ
My lord, you must tell us where the body is and go with us to the king.

HAMLET
The body is with the king, but the king is not with the body. The king is a thing,—

GUILDENSTERN
A thing, my lord!

HAMLET
Of nothing: bring me to him. Hide fox, and all after.

[Exeunt.]

Scene III. Another room in the Castle.

[Enter King, attended.]

KING
I have sent to seek him and to find the body.
How dangerous is it that this man goes loose!
Yet must not we put the strong law on him:
He's lov'd of the distracted multitude,
Who like not in their judgment, but their eyes;
And where 'tis so, the offender's scourge is weigh'd,
But never the offence. To bear all smooth and even,
This sudden sending him away must seem
Deliberate pause: diseases desperate grown
By desperate appliance are reliev'd,
Or not at all.

[Enter Rosencrantz.]

How now! what hath befall'n?

ROSENCRANTZ
Where the dead body is bestow'd, my lord,
We cannot get from him.

KING
But where is he?

ROSENCRANTZ
Without, my lord; guarded, to know your pleasure.

KING
Bring him before us.

ROSENCRANTZ
Ho, Guildenstern! bring in my lord.
[Enter Hamlet and Guildenstern.]

KING
Now, Hamlet, where's Polonius?

HAMLET
At supper.

KING
At supper! where?

HAMLET
Not where he eats, but where he is eaten: a certain convocation of
politic worms are e'en at him. Your worm is your only emperor
for diet: we fat all creatures else to fat us, and we fat ourselves
for maggots: your fat king and your lean beggar is but variable
service,—two dishes, but to one table: that's the end.

KING
Alas, alas!

HAMLET
A man may fish with the worm that hath eat of a king, and eat of
the fish that hath fed of that worm.

KING
What dost thou mean by this?

HAMLET
Nothing but to show you how a king may go a progress through the guts of a beggar.

KING
Where is Polonius?

HAMLET
In heaven: send thither to see: if your messenger find him not there, seek him i' the other place yourself. But, indeed, if you find him not within this month, you shall nose him as you go up the stairs into the lobby.

KING
Go seek him there. *[To some Attendants.]*

HAMLET
He will stay till you come.

[Exeunt Attendants.]

KING
Hamlet, this deed, for thine especial safety,—
Which we do tender, as we dearly grieve
For that which thou hast done,—must send thee hence
With fiery quickness: therefore prepare thyself;
The bark is ready, and the wind at help,
The associates tend, and everything is bent
For England.

HAMLET
For England!

KING
Ay, Hamlet.

HAMLET
Good.

KING
So is it, if thou knew'st our purposes.

HAMLET
I see a cherub that sees them.—But, come; for England!—
Farewell, dear mother.

KING
Thy loving father, Hamlet.

HAMLET
My mother: father and mother is man and wife; man and wife is
one flesh; and so, my mother.—Come, for England!

[Exit.]

KING
Follow him at foot; tempt him with speed aboard;
Delay it not; I'll have him hence to-night:
Away! for everything is seal'd and done
That else leans on the affair: pray you, make haste.

[Exeunt Rosencrantz and Guildenstern.]

And, England, if my love thou hold'st at aught,—
As my great power thereof may give thee sense,
Since yet thy cicatrice looks raw and red
After the Danish sword, and thy free awe
Pays homage to us,—thou mayst not coldly set
Our sovereign process; which imports at full,
By letters conjuring to that effect,
The present death of Hamlet. Do it, England;
For like the hectic in my blood he rages,
And thou must cure me: till I know 'tis done,
Howe'er my haps, my joys were ne'er begun.

[Exit.]

Scene IV. A plain in Denmark.

[Enter Fortinbras, and Forces marching.]

FORTINBRAS
Go, Captain, from me greet the Danish king:
Tell him that, by his license, Fortinbras
Craves the conveyance of a promis'd march
Over his kingdom. You know the rendezvous.
If that his majesty would aught with us,
We shall express our duty in his eye;
And let him know so.

CAPTAIN
I will do't, my lord.

FORTINBRAS
Go softly on.

[Exeunt all Fortinbras and Forces.]

[Enter Hamlet, Rosencrantz, Guildenstern, and others.]

HAMLET
Good sir, whose powers are these?

CAPTAIN
They are of Norway, sir.

HAMLET
How purpos'd, sir, I pray you?

CAPTAIN
Against some part of Poland.

HAMLET
Who commands them, sir?

CAPTAIN
The nephew to old Norway, Fortinbras.

HAMLET
Goes it against the main of Poland, sir,
Or for some frontier?

CAPTAIN
Truly to speak, and with no addition,

We go to gain a little patch of ground
That hath in it no profit but the name.
To pay five ducats, five, I would not farm it;
Nor will it yield to Norway or the Pole
A ranker rate, should it be sold in fee.

HAMLET
Why, then the Polack never will defend it.

CAPTAIN
Yes, it is already garrison'd.

HAMLET
Two thousand souls and twenty thousand ducats
Will not debate the question of this straw:
This is the imposthume of much wealth and peace,
That inward breaks, and shows no cause without
Why the man dies.—I humbly thank you, sir.
CAPTAIN
God b' wi' you, sir.

[Exit.]

ROSENCRANTZ
Will't please you go, my lord?

HAMLET
I'll be with you straight. Go a little before.

[Exeunt all but Hamlet.]

How all occasions do inform against me
And spur my dull revenge! What is a man,
If his chief good and market of his time
Be but to sleep and feed? a beast, no more.
Sure he that made us with such large discourse,
Looking before and after, gave us not
That capability and godlike reason
To fust in us unus'd. Now, whether it be
Bestial oblivion, or some craven scruple
Of thinking too precisely on the event,—

A thought which, quarter'd, hath but one part wisdom
And ever three parts coward,—I do not know
Why yet I live to say 'This thing's to do;'
Sith I have cause, and will, and strength, and means
To do't. Examples, gross as earth, exhort me:
Witness this army, of such mass and charge,
Led by a delicate and tender prince;
Whose spirit, with divine ambition puff'd,
Makes mouths at the invisible event;
Exposing what is mortal and unsure
To all that fortune, death, and danger dare,
Even for an egg-shell. Rightly to be great
Is not to stir without great argument,
But greatly to find quarrel in a straw
When honour's at the stake. How stand I, then,
That have a father kill'd, a mother stain'd,
Excitements of my reason and my blood,
And let all sleep? while, to my shame, I see
The imminent death of twenty thousand men
That, for a fantasy and trick of fame,
Go to their graves like beds; fight for a plot
Whereon the numbers cannot try the cause,
Which is not tomb enough and continent
To hide the slain?—O, from this time forth,
My thoughts be bloody, or be nothing worth!

[Exit.]

Scene V. Elsinore. A room in the Castle.

[Enter Queen and Horatio.]

QUEEN
I will not speak with her.

GENTLEMAN
She is importunate; indeed distract:
Her mood will needs be pitied.

QUEEN
What would she have?

GENTLEMAN
She speaks much of her father; says she hears
There's tricks i' the world, and hems, and beats her heart;
Spurns enviously at straws; speaks things in doubt,
That carry but half sense: her speech is nothing,
Yet the unshaped use of it doth move
The hearers to collection; they aim at it,
And botch the words up fit to their own thoughts;
Which, as her winks, and nods, and gestures yield them,
Indeed would make one think there might be thought,
Though nothing sure, yet much unhappily.
'Twere good she were spoken with; for she may strew
Dangerous conjectures in ill-breeding minds.

QUEEN
Let her come in.
[Exit Horatio.]

To my sick soul, as sin's true nature is,
Each toy seems Prologue to some great amiss:
So full of artless jealousy is guilt,
It spills itself in fearing to be spilt.

[Re-enter Horatio with Ophelia.]

OPHELIA
Where is the beauteous majesty of Denmark?

QUEEN
How now, Ophelia?

OPHELIA
[Sings.]
    How should I your true love know
        From another one?
    By his cockle bat and' staff
        And his sandal shoon.

QUEEN
Alas, sweet lady, what imports this song?

OPHELIA
Say you? nay, pray you, mark.
[Sings.]
    He is dead and gone, lady,
      He is dead and gone;
    At his head a grass green turf,
      At his heels a stone.

QUEEN
Nay, but Ophelia—

OPHELIA
Pray you, mark.
[Sings.]
    White his shroud as the mountain snow,

[Enter King.]
QUEEN
Alas, look here, my lord!

OPHELIA
[Sings.]
    Larded all with sweet flowers;
    Which bewept to the grave did go
      With true-love showers.

KING
How do you, pretty lady?

OPHELIA
Well, God dild you! They say the owl was a baker's daughter. Lord, we know what we are, but know not what we may be. God be at your table!

KING
Conceit upon her father.

OPHELIA
Pray you, let's have no words of this; but when they ask you what it means, say you this:
[Sings.]
> To-morrow is Saint Valentine's day
> > All in the morning bedtime,
> And I a maid at your window,
> > To be your Valentine.
>
> Then up he rose and donn'd his clothes,
> > And dupp'd the chamber door,
> Let in the maid, that out a maid
> > Never departed more.

KING
Pretty Ophelia!

OPHELIA
Indeed, la, without an oath, I'll make an end on't:
[Sings.]
> By Gis and by Saint Charity,
> > Alack, and fie for shame!
> Young men will do't if they come to't;
> > By cock, they are to blame.
>
> Quoth she, before you tumbled me,
> > You promis'd me to wed.
> So would I ha' done, by yonder sun,
> > An thou hadst not come to my bed.

KING
How long hath she been thus?

OPHELIA
I hope all will be well. We must be patient: but I cannot choose but weep, to think they would lay him i' the cold ground. My brother shall know of it: and so I thank you for your good counsel.— Come, my coach!—Good night, ladies; good night, sweet ladies; good night, good night.

[Exit.]

KING
Follow her close; give her good watch, I pray you.

[Exit Horatio.]

O, this is the poison of deep grief; it springs
All from her father's death. O Gertrude, Gertrude,
When sorrows come, they come not single spies,
But in battalions! First, her father slain:
Next, your son gone; and he most violent author
Of his own just remove: the people muddied,
Thick and and unwholesome in their thoughts and whispers
For good Polonius' death; and we have done but greenly
In hugger-mugger to inter him: poor Ophelia
Divided from herself and her fair judgment,
Without the which we are pictures or mere beasts:
Last, and as much containing as all these,
Her brother is in secret come from France;
Feeds on his wonder, keeps himself in clouds,
And wants not buzzers to infect his ear
With pestilent speeches of his father's death;
Wherein necessity, of matter beggar'd,
Will nothing stick our person to arraign
In ear and ear. O my dear Gertrude, this,
Like to a murdering piece, in many places
Give, me superfluous death.

[A noise within.]

QUEEN
Alack, what noise is this?

KING
Where are my Switzers? let them guard the door.

[Enter a Gentleman.]

What is the matter?

GENTLEMAN
Save yourself, my lord:

The ocean, overpeering of his list,
Eats not the flats with more impetuous haste
Than young Laertes, in a riotous head,
O'erbears your offices. The rabble call him lord;
And, as the world were now but to begin,
Antiquity forgot, custom not known,
The ratifiers and props of every word,
They cry 'Choose we! Laertes shall be king!'
Caps, hands, and tongues applaud it to the clouds,
'Laertes shall be king! Laertes king!'

QUEEN
How cheerfully on the false trail they cry!
O, this is counter, you false Danish dogs!

[A noise within.]

KING
The doors are broke.

[Enter Laertes, armed; Danes following.]

LAERTES
Where is this king?—Sirs, stand you all without.

DANES
No, let's come in.

LAERTES
I pray you, give me leave.

DANES
We will, we will.

[They retire without the door.]

LAERTES
I thank you:—keep the door.—O thou vile king,
Give me my father!

QUEEN
Calmly, good Laertes.

LAERTES
That drop of blood that's calm proclaims me bastard;
Cries cuckold to my father; brands the harlot
Even here, between the chaste unsmirched brow
Of my true mother.

KING
What is the cause, Laertes,
That thy rebellion looks so giant-like?—
Let him go, Gertrude; do not fear our person:
There's such divinity doth hedge a king,
That treason can but peep to what it would,
Acts little of his will.—Tell me, Laertes,
Why thou art thus incens'd.—Let him go, Gertrude:—
Speak, man.

LAERTES
Where is my father?

KING
Dead.
QUEEN
But not by him.

KING
Let him demand his fill.

LAERTES
How came he dead? I'll not be juggled with:
To hell, allegiance! vows, to the blackest devil!
Conscience and grace, to the profoundest pit!
I dare damnation:—to this point I stand,—
That both the worlds, I give to negligence,
Let come what comes; only I'll be reveng'd
Most throughly for my father.

KING
Who shall stay you?

LAERTES
My will, not all the world:
And for my means, I'll husband them so well,
They shall go far with little.

KING
Good Laertes,
If you desire to know the certainty
Of your dear father's death, is't writ in your revenge
That, sweepstake, you will draw both friend and foe,
Winner and loser?

LAERTES
None but his enemies.

KING
Will you know them then?

LAERTES
To his good friends thus wide I'll ope my arms;
And, like the kind life-rendering pelican,
Repast them with my blood.

KING
Why, now you speak
Like a good child and a true gentleman.
That I am guiltless of your father's death,
And am most sensibly in grief for it,
It shall as level to your judgment pierce
As day does to your eye.

DANES
[Within] Let her come in.

LAERTES
How now! What noise is that?

[Re-enter Ophelia, fantastically dressed with straws and flowers.]

O heat, dry up my brains! tears seven times salt,
Burn out the sense and virtue of mine eye!—

By heaven, thy madness shall be paid by weight,
Till our scale turn the beam. O rose of May!
Dear maid, kind sister, sweet Ophelia!—
O heavens! is't possible a young maid's wits
Should be as mortal as an old man's life?
Nature is fine in love; and where 'tis fine,
It sends some precious instance of itself
After the thing it loves.

OPHELIA
[Sings.]
    They bore him barefac'd on the bier
    Hey no nonny, nonny, hey nonny
    And on his grave rain'd many a tear.—

Fare you well, my dove!

LAERTES
Hadst thou thy wits, and didst persuade revenge,
It could not move thus.

OPHELIA
You must sing 'Down a-down, an you call him a-down-a.' O, how
the wheel becomes it! It is the false steward, that stole his master's
daughter.

LAERTES
This nothing's more than matter.

OPHELIA
There's rosemary, that's for remembrance; pray, love, remember:
and there is pansies, that's for thoughts.

LAERTES
A document in madness,—thoughts and remembrance fitted.

OPHELIA
There's fennel for you, and columbines:—there's rue for you; and
here's some for me:—we may call it herb of grace o' Sundays:—
O, you must wear your rue with a difference.—There's a daisy:—
I would give you some violets, but they wither'd all when my

father died:—they say he made a good end,— *[Sings.]* For bonny
sweet Robin is all my joy,—

LAERTES
Thought and affliction, passion, hell itself,
She turns to favour and to prettiness.

OPHELIA
[Sings.]
> And will he not come again?
> And will he not come again?
>> No, no, he is dead,
>> Go to thy death-bed,
> He never will come again.

> His beard was as white as snow,
> All flaxen was his poll:
>> He is gone, he is gone,
>> And we cast away moan:
> God ha' mercy on his soul!

And of all Christian souls, I pray God.—God b' wi' ye.

[Exit.]

LAERTES
Do you see this, O God?

KING
Laertes, I must commune with your grief,
Or you deny me right. Go but apart,
Make choice of whom your wisest friends you will,
And they shall hear and judge 'twixt you and me.
If by direct or by collateral hand
They find us touch'd, we will our kingdom give,
Our crown, our life, and all that we call ours,
To you in satisfaction; but if not,
Be you content to lend your patience to us,
And we shall jointly labour with your soul
To give it due content.

LAERTES
Let this be so;
His means of death, his obscure burial,—
No trophy, sword, nor hatchment o'er his bones,
No noble rite nor formal ostentation,—
Cry to be heard, as 'twere from heaven to earth,
That I must call't in question.

KING
So you shall;
And where the offence is let the great axe fall.
I pray you go with me.

[Exeunt.]

Scene VI. Another room in the Castle.

[Enter Horatio and a Servant.]

HORATIO
What are they that would speak with me?

SERVANT
Sailors, sir: they say they have letters for you.

HORATIO
Let them come in.

[Exit Servant.]

I do not know from what part of the world
I should be greeted, if not from Lord Hamlet.

[Enter Sailors.]

I SAILOR
God bless you, sir.

HORATIO
Let him bless thee too.

SAILOR
He shall, sir, an't please him. There's a letter for you, sir,—it comes

from the ambassador that was bound for England; if your name
be Horatio, as I am let to know it is.

HORATIO
[Reads.] 'Horatio, when thou shalt have overlooked this, give
these fellows some means to the king: they have letters for him.
Ere we were two days old at sea, a pirate of very warlike appoint-
ment gave us chase. Finding ourselves too slow of sail, we put
on a compelled valour, and in the grapple I boarded them: on
the instant they got clear of our ship; so I alone became their
prisoner. They have dealt with me like thieves of mercy: but they
knew what they did; I am to do a good turn for them. Let the
king have the letters I have sent; and repair thou to me with as
much haste as thou wouldst fly death. I have words to speak in
thine ear will make thee dumb; yet are they much too light for
the bore of the matter. These good fellows will bring thee where I
am. Rosencrantz and Guildenstern hold their course for England:
of them I have much to tell thee. Farewell. He that thou knowest
thine, HAMLET.'

Come, I will give you way for these your letters;
And do't the speedier, that you may direct me
To him from whom you brought them.

[Exeunt.]

Scene VII. Another room in the Castle.

[Enter King and Laertes.]

KING
Now must your conscience my acquittance seal,
And you must put me in your heart for friend,
Sith you have heard, and with a knowing ear,
That he which hath your noble father slain
Pursu'd my life.

LAERTES
It well appears:—but tell me
Why you proceeded not against these feats,

So crimeful and so capital in nature,
As by your safety, wisdom, all things else,
You mainly were stirr'd up.

KING
O, for two special reasons;
Which may to you, perhaps, seem much unsinew'd,
But yet to me they are strong. The queen his mother
Lives almost by his looks; and for myself,—
My virtue or my plague, be it either which,—
She's so conjunctive to my life and soul,
That, as the star moves not but in his sphere,
I could not but by her. The other motive,
Why to a public count I might not go,
Is the great love the general gender bear him;
Who, dipping all his faults in their affection,
Would, like the spring that turneth wood to stone,
Convert his gyves to graces; so that my arrows,
Too slightly timber'd for so loud a wind,
Would have reverted to my bow again,
And not where I had aim'd them.

LAERTES
And so have I a noble father lost;
A sister driven into desperate terms,—
Whose worth, if praises may go back again,
Stood challenger on mount of all the age
For her perfections:—but my revenge will come.

KING
Break not your sleeps for that:—you must not think
That we are made of stuff so flat and dull
That we can let our beard be shook with danger,
And think it pastime. You shortly shall hear more:
I lov'd your father, and we love ourself;
And that, I hope, will teach you to imagine,—

[Enter a Messenger.]

How now! What news?

MESSENGER
Letters, my lord, from Hamlet:
This to your majesty; this to the queen.

KING
From Hamlet! Who brought them?

MESSENGER
Sailors, my lord, they say; I saw them not:
They were given me by Claudio:—he receiv'd them
Of him that brought them.

KING
Laertes, you shall hear them.
Leave us.

[Exit Messenger.]

[Reads] 'High and mighty,—You shall know I am set naked on your kingdom. To-morrow shall I beg leave to see your kingly eyes: when I shall, first asking your pardon thereunto, recount the occasions of my sudden and more strange return. HAMLET.'

What should this mean? Are all the rest come back?
Or is it some abuse, and no such thing?

LAERTES
Know you the hand?

KING
'Tis Hamlet's character:—'Naked!'—
And in a postscript here, he says 'alone.'
Can you advise me?

LAERTES
I am lost in it, my lord. But let him come;
It warms the very sickness in my heart
That I shall live and tell him to his teeth,
'Thus didest thou.'

KING
If it be so, Laertes,—

As how should it be so? how otherwise?—
Will you be rul'd by me?

LAERTES
Ay, my lord;
So you will not o'errule me to a peace.

KING
To thine own peace. If he be now return'd—
As checking at his voyage, and that he means
No more to undertake it,—I will work him
To exploit, now ripe in my device,
Under the which he shall not choose but fall:
And for his death no wind shall breathe;
But even his mother shall uncharge the practice
And call it accident.

LAERTES
My lord, I will be rul'd;
The rather if you could devise it so
That I might be the organ.

KING
It falls right.
You have been talk'd of since your travel much,
And that in Hamlet's hearing, for a quality
Wherein they say you shine: your sum of parts
Did not together pluck such envy from him
As did that one; and that, in my regard,
Of the unworthiest siege.

LAERTES
What part is that, my lord?

KING
A very riband in the cap of youth,
Yet needful too; for youth no less becomes
The light and careless livery that it wears
Than settled age his sables and his weeds,

Importing health and graveness.—Two months since,
Here was a gentleman of Normandy,—
I've seen myself, and serv'd against, the French,
And they can well on horseback: but this gallant
Had witchcraft in't: he grew unto his seat;
And to such wondrous doing brought his horse,
As had he been incorps'd and demi-natur'd
With the brave beast: so far he topp'd my thought
That I, in forgery of shapes and tricks,
Come short of what he did.

LAERTES
A Norman was't?

KING
A Norman.

LAERTES
Upon my life, Lamond.

KING
The very same.

LAERTES
I know him well: he is the brooch indeed
And gem of all the nation.

KING
He made confession of you;
And gave you such a masterly report
For art and exercise in your defence,
And for your rapier most especially,
That he cried out, 'twould be a sight indeed
If one could match you: the scrimers of their nation
He swore, had neither motion, guard, nor eye,
If you oppos'd them. Sir, this report of his
Did Hamlet so envenom with his envy
That he could nothing do but wish and beg
Your sudden coming o'er, to play with him.
Now, out of this,—

LAERTES
What out of this, my lord?

KING
Laertes, was your father dear to you?
Or are you like the painting of a sorrow,
A face without a heart?

LAERTES
Why ask you this?

KING
Not that I think you did not love your father;
But that I know love is begun by time,
And that I see, in passages of proof,
Time qualifies the spark and fire of it.
There lives within the very flame of love
A kind of wick or snuff that will abate it;
And nothing is at a like goodness still;
For goodness, growing to a plurisy,
Dies in his own too much: that we would do,
We should do when we would; for this 'would' changes,
And hath abatements and delays as many
As there are tongues, are hands, are accidents;
And then this 'should' is like a spendthrift sigh,
That hurts by easing. But to the quick o' the ulcer:—
Hamlet comes back: what would you undertake
To show yourself your father's son in deed
More than in words?

LAERTES
To cut his throat i' the church.

KING
No place, indeed, should murder sanctuarize;
Revenge should have no bounds. But, good Laertes,
Will you do this, keep close within your chamber.
Hamlet return'd shall know you are come home:
We'll put on those shall praise your excellence

And set a double varnish on the fame
The Frenchman gave you; bring you in fine together
And wager on your heads: he, being remiss,
Most generous, and free from all contriving,
Will not peruse the foils; so that with ease,
Or with a little shuffling, you may choose
A sword unbated, and, in a pass of practice,
Requite him for your father.

LAERTES
I will do't:
And for that purpose I'll anoint my sword.
I bought an unction of a mountebank,
So mortal that, but dip a knife in it,
Where it draws blood no cataplasm so rare,
Collected from all simples that have virtue
Under the moon, can save the thing from death
This is but scratch'd withal: I'll touch my point
With this contagion, that, if I gall him slightly,
It may be death.

KING
Let's further think of this;
Weigh what convenience both of time and means
May fit us to our shape: if this should fail,
And that our drift look through our bad performance.
'Twere better not assay'd: therefore this project
Should have a back or second, that might hold
If this did blast in proof. Soft! let me see:—
We'll make a solemn wager on your cunnings,—
I ha't:
When in your motion you are hot and dry,—
As make your bouts more violent to that end,—
And that he calls for drink, I'll have prepar'd him
A chalice for the nonce; whereon but sipping,
If he by chance escape your venom'd stuck,
Our purpose may hold there.

[Enter Queen.]

How now, sweet queen!

QUEEN
One woe doth tread upon another's heel,
So fast they follow:—your sister's drown'd, Laertes.

LAERTES
Drown'd! O, where?

QUEEN
There is a willow grows aslant a brook,
That shows his hoar leaves in the glassy stream;
There with fantastic garlands did she come
Of crowflowers, nettles, daisies, and long purples,
That liberal shepherds give a grosser name,
But our cold maids do dead men's fingers call them.
There, on the pendant boughs her coronet weeds
Clamb'ring to hang, an envious sliver broke;
When down her weedy trophies and herself
Fell in the weeping brook. Her clothes spread wide;
And, mermaid-like, awhile they bore her up;
Which time she chaunted snatches of old tunes;
As one incapable of her own distress,
Or like a creature native and indu'd
Unto that element: but long it could not be
Till that her garments, heavy with their drink,
Pull'd the poor wretch from her melodious lay
To muddy death.

LAERTES
Alas, then she is drown'd?

QUEEN
Drown'd, drown'd.

LAERTES
Too much of water hast thou, poor Ophelia,
And therefore I forbid my tears: but yet

It is our trick; nature her custom holds,
Let shame say what it will: when these are gone,
The woman will be out.—Adieu, my lord:
I have a speech of fire, that fain would blaze,
But that this folly douts it.

[Exit.]

KING
Let's follow, Gertrude;
How much I had to do to calm his rage!
Now fear I this will give it start again;
Therefore let's follow.

[Exeunt.]

ACT V

Scene I. A churchyard.

[Enter two Clowns, with spades, etc.]

1 CLOWN
Is she to be buried in Christian burial when she wilfully seeks her
own salvation?

2 CLOWN
I tell thee she is; and therefore make her grave straight: the crowner
hath sat on her, and finds it Christian burial.

1 CLOWN
How can that be, unless she drowned herself in her own
defence?

2 CLOWN
Why, 'tis found so.

1 CLOWN
It must be se offendendo; it cannot be else. For here lies the point:
if I drown myself wittingly, it argues an act: and an act hath three
branches; it is to act, to do, and to perform: argal, she drowned
herself wittingly.

2 CLOWN
Nay, but hear you, goodman delver,—

1 CLOWN
Give me leave. Here lies the water; good: here stands the man; good: if the man go to this water and drown himself, it is, will he, nill he, he goes,—mark you that: but if the water come to him and drown him, he drowns not himself; argal, he that is not guilty of his own death shortens not his own life.

2 CLOWN
But is this law?

1 CLOWN
Ay, marry, is't—crowner's quest law.

2 CLOWN
Will you ha' the truth on't? If this had not been a gentlewoman, she should have been buried out o' Christian burial.

1 CLOWN
Why, there thou say'st: and the more pity that great folk should have countenance in this world to drown or hang themselves more than their even Christian.—Come, my spade. There is no ancient gentlemen but gardeners, ditchers, and grave-makers: they hold up Adam's profession.

2 CLOWN
Was he a gentleman?

1 CLOWN
He was the first that ever bore arms.

2 CLOWN
Why, he had none.

1 CLOWN
What, art a heathen? How dost thou understand the Scripture? The Scripture says Adam digg'd: could he dig without arms? I'll put another question to thee: if thou answerest me not to the purpose, confess thyself,—

2 CLOWN

Go to.

1 CLOWN

What is he that builds stronger than either the mason, the ship-wright, or the carpenter?

2 CLOWN

The gallows-maker; for that frame outlives a thousand tenants.

1 CLOWN

I like thy wit well, in good faith: the gallows does well; but how does it well? it does well to those that do ill: now, thou dost ill to say the gallows is built stronger than the church; argal, the gallows may do well to thee. To't again, come.

2 CLOWN

Who builds stronger than a mason, a shipwright, or a carpenter?

1 CLOWN

Ay, tell me that, and unyoke.

2 CLOWN

Marry, now I can tell.

1 CLOWN

To't.

2 CLOWN

Mass, I cannot tell.

[Enter Hamlet and Horatio, at a distance.]

1 CLOWN

Cudgel thy brains no more about it, for your dull ass will not mend his pace with beating; and when you are asked this question next, say 'a grave-maker;' the houses he makes last till doomsday. Go, get thee to Yaughan; fetch me a stoup of liquor.

[Exit Second Clown.]

[Digs and sings.]

In youth when I did love, did love,
    Methought it was very sweet;
To contract, O, the time for, ah, my behove,
    O, methought there was nothing meet.

HAMLET
Has this fellow no feeling of his business, that he sings at grave-making?

HORATIO
Custom hath made it in him a property of easiness.

HAMLET
'Tis e'en so: the hand of little employment hath the daintier sense.

1 CLOWN
[Sings.]
    But age, with his stealing steps,
        Hath claw'd me in his clutch,
    And hath shipp'd me into the land,
        As if I had never been such.
[Throws up a skull.]

HAMLET
That skull had a tongue in it, and could sing once: how the knave jowls it to the ground, as if 'twere Cain's jawbone, that did the first murder! This might be the pate of a politician, which this ass now o'erreaches; one that would circumvent God, might it not?

HORATIO
It might, my lord.

HAMLET
Or of a courtier, which could say 'Good morrow, sweet lord! How dost thou, good lord?' This might be my lord such-a-one, that praised my lord such-a-one's horse when he meant to beg it,—might it not?

HORATIO
Ay, my lord.

HAMLET

Why, e'en so: and now my Lady Worm's; chapless, and knocked about the mazard with a sexton's spade: here's fine revolution, an we had the trick to see't. Did these bones cost no more the breeding but to play at loggets with 'em? mine ache to think on't.

1 CLOWN

[Sings.]

> A pickaxe and a spade, a spade,
>> For and a shrouding sheet;
> O, a pit of clay for to be made
>> For such a guest is meet.

[Throws up another skull.]

HAMLET

There's another: why may not that be the skull of a lawyer? Where be his quiddits now, his quillets, his cases, his tenures, and his tricks? why does he suffer this rude knave now to knock him about the sconce with a dirty shovel, and will not tell him of his action of battery? Hum! This fellow might be in's time a great buyer of land, with his statutes, his recognizances, his fines, his double vouchers, his recoveries: is this the fine of his fines, and the recovery of his recoveries, to have his fine pate full of fine dirt? will his vouchers vouch him no more of his purchases, and double ones too, than the length and breadth of a pair of indentures? The very conveyances of his lands will scarcely lie in this box; and must the inheritor himself have no more, ha?

HORATIO

Not a jot more, my lord.

HAMLET

Is not parchment made of sheep-skins?

HORATIO

Ay, my lord, And of calf-skins too.

HAMLET

They are sheep and calves which seek out assurance in that. I will speak to this fellow.—Whose grave's this, sir?

1 CLOWN
Mine, sir.
[Sings.]
> O, a pit of clay for to be made
> > For such a guest is meet.

HAMLET
I think it be thine indeed, for thou liest in't.

1 CLOWN
You lie out on't, sir, and therefore 'tis not yours: for my part, I do not lie in't, yet it is mine.

HAMLET
Thou dost lie in't, to be in't and say it is thine: 'tis for the dead, not for the quick; therefore thou liest.

1 CLOWN
'Tis a quick lie, sir; 't will away again from me to you.

HAMLET
What man dost thou dig it for?
1 CLOWN
For no man, sir.

HAMLET
What woman then?

1 CLOWN
For none neither.

HAMLET
Who is to be buried in't?

1 CLOWN
One that was a woman, sir; but, rest her soul, she's dead.

HAMLET
How absolute the knave is! We must speak by the card, or equivocation will undo us. By the Lord, Horatio, these three years I have taken note of it, the age is grown so picked that the toe of the peasant comes so near the heel of the courtier he galls his kibe.— How long hast thou been a grave-maker?

1 CLOWN

Of all the days i' the year, I came to't that day that our last King Hamlet overcame Fortinbras.

HAMLET

How long is that since?

1 CLOWN

Cannot you tell that? every fool can tell that: it was the very day that young Hamlet was born,—he that is mad, and sent into England.

HAMLET

Ay, marry, why was be sent into England?

1 CLOWN

Why, because he was mad: he shall recover his wits there; or, if he do not, it's no great matter there.

HAMLET

Why?

1 CLOWN

'Twill not he seen in him there; there the men are as mad as he.

HAMLET

How came he mad?

1 CLOWN

Very strangely, they say.

HAMLET

How strangely?

1 CLOWN

Faith, e'en with losing his wits.

HAMLET

Upon what ground?

1 CLOWN

Why, here in Denmark: I have been sexton here, man and boy, thirty years.

HAMLET
How long will a man lie i' the earth ere he rot?

1 CLOWN
Faith, if he be not rotten before he die,—as we have many pocky corses now-a-days that will scarce hold the laying in,—he will last you some eight year or nine year: a tanner will last you nine year.

HAMLET
Why he more than another?

1 CLOWN
Why, sir, his hide is so tann'd with his trade that he will keep out water a great while; and your water is a sore decayer of your whoreson dead body. Here's a skull now; this skull hath lain in the earth three-and-twenty years.

HAMLET
Whose was it?

1 CLOWN
A whoreson, mad fellow's it was: whose do you think it was?

HAMLET
Nay, I know not.

1 CLOWN
A pestilence on him for a mad rogue! 'a pour'd a flagon of Rhenish on my head once. This same skull, sir, was Yorick's skull, the king's jester.

HAMLET
This?

1 CLOWN
E'en that.

HAMLET
Let me see. *[Takes the skull.]* Alas, poor Yorick!—I knew him, Horatio; a fellow of infinite jest, of most excellent fancy: he hath borne me on his back a thousand times; and now, how abhorred in my

imagination it is! my gorge rises at it. Here hung those lips that I have kiss'd I know not how oft. Where be your gibes now? your gambols? your songs? your flashes of merriment, that were wont to set the table on a roar? Not one now, to mock your own grinning? quite chap-fallen? Now, get you to my lady's chamber, and tell her, let her paint an inch thick, to this favour she must come; make her laugh at that.—Pr'ythee, Horatio, tell me one thing.

HORATIO
What's that, my lord?

HAMLET
Dost thou think Alexander looked o' this fashion i' the earth?

HORATIO
E'en so.

HAMLET
And smelt so? Pah!

[Throws down the skull.]

HORATIO
E'en so, my lord.

HAMLET
To what base uses we may return, Horatio! Why may not imagination trace the noble dust of Alexander till he find it stopping a bung-hole?

HORATIO
'Twere to consider too curiously to consider so.

HAMLET
No, faith, not a jot; but to follow him thither with modesty enough, and likelihood to lead it: as thus: Alexander died, Alexander was buried, Alexander returneth into dust; the dust is earth; of earth we make loam; and why of that loam whereto he was converted might they not stop a beer-barrel?

    Imperious Caesar, dead and turn'd to clay,
    Might stop a hole to keep the wind away.

O, that that earth which kept the world in awe
  Should patch a wall to expel the winter's flaw!
But soft! but soft! aside!—Here comes the king.

*[Enter priests, etc., in procession; the corpse of Ophelia, Laertes,
and Mourners following; King, Queen, their Trains, etc.]*

The queen, the courtiers: who is that they follow?
And with such maimed rites? This doth betoken
The corse they follow did with desperate hand
Fordo it own life: 'twas of some estate.
Couch we awhile and mark.

[Retiring with Horatio.]

LAERTES
What ceremony else?

HAMLET
That is Laertes,
A very noble youth: mark.
LAERTES
What ceremony else?

1 PRIEST
Her obsequies have been as far enlarg'd
As we have warranties: her death was doubtful;
And, but that great command o'ersways the order,
She should in ground unsanctified have lodg'd
Till the last trumpet; for charitable prayers,
Shards, flints, and pebbles should be thrown on her,
Yet here she is allowed her virgin rites,
Her maiden strewments, and the bringing home
Of bell and burial.

LAERTES
Must there no more be done?

1 PRIEST
No more be done;
We should profane the service of the dead

To sing a requiem and such rest to her
As to peace-parted souls.

LAERTES
Lay her i' the earth;—
And from her fair and unpolluted flesh
May violets spring!—I tell thee, churlish priest,
A ministering angel shall my sister be
When thou liest howling.

HAMLET
What, the fair Ophelia?

QUEEN
Sweets to the sweet: farewell.
[Scattering flowers.]
I hop'd thou shouldst have been my Hamlet's wife;
I thought thy bride-bed to have deck'd, sweet maid,
And not have strew'd thy grave.

LAERTES
O, treble woe
Fall ten times treble on that cursed head
Whose wicked deed thy most ingenious sense
Depriv'd thee of!—Hold off the earth awhile,
Till I have caught her once more in mine arms:
[Leaps into the grave.]
Now pile your dust upon the quick and dead,
Till of this flat a mountain you have made,
To o'ertop old Pelion or the skyish head
Of blue Olympus.

HAMLET
[Advancing.]
What is he whose grief
Bears such an emphasis? whose phrase of sorrow
Conjures the wandering stars, and makes them stand
Like wonder-wounded hearers? this is I,
Hamlet the Dane.

[Leaps into the grave.]

LAERTES
The devil take thy soul!
[Grappling with him.]

HAMLET
Thou pray'st not well.
I pr'ythee, take thy fingers from my throat;
For, though I am not splenetive and rash,
Yet have I in me something dangerous,
Which let thy wiseness fear: away thy hand!

KING
Pluck them asunder.

QUEEN
Hamlet! Hamlet!

ALL
Gentlemen!—

HORATIO
Good my lord, be quiet.

[The Attendants part them, and they come out of the grave.]

HAMLET
Why, I will fight with him upon this theme
Until my eyelids will no longer wag.

QUEEN
O my son, what theme?

HAMLET
I lov'd Ophelia; forty thousand brothers
Could not, with all their quantity of love,
Make up my sum.—What wilt thou do for her?

KING
O, he is mad, Laertes.

QUEEN
For love of God, forbear him!

HAMLET
'Swounds, show me what thou'lt do:
Woul't weep? woul't fight? woul't fast? woul't tear thyself?
Woul't drink up eisel? eat a crocodile?
I'll do't.—Dost thou come here to whine?
To outface me with leaping in her grave?
Be buried quick with her, and so will I:
And, if thou prate of mountains, let them throw
Millions of acres on us, till our ground,
Singeing his pate against the burning zone,
Make Ossa like a wart! Nay, an thou'lt mouth,
I'll rant as well as thou.

QUEEN
This is mere madness:
And thus a while the fit will work on him;
Anon, as patient as the female dove,
When that her golden couplets are disclos'd,
His silence will sit drooping.

HAMLET
Hear you, sir;
What is the reason that you use me thus?
I lov'd you ever: but it is no matter;
Let Hercules himself do what he may,
The cat will mew, and dog will have his day.

[Exit.]

KING
I pray thee, good Horatio, wait upon him.—

[Exit Horatio.]

[To Laertes]
Strengthen your patience in our last night's speech;
We'll put the matter to the present push.—
Good Gertrude, set some watch over your son.—
This grave shall have a living monument:

An hour of quiet shortly shall we see;
Till then in patience our proceeding be.

[Exeunt.]

Scene II. A hall in the Castle.

[Enter Hamlet and Horatio.]

HAMLET
So much for this, sir: now let me see the other;
You do remember all the circumstance?

HORATIO
Remember it, my lord!

HAMLET
Sir, in my heart there was a kind of fighting
That would not let me sleep: methought I lay
Worse than the mutinies in the bilboes. Rashly,
And prais'd be rashness for it,—let us know,
Our indiscretion sometime serves us well,
When our deep plots do fail; and that should teach us
There's a divinity that shapes our ends,
Rough-hew them how we will.

HORATIO
That is most certain.

HAMLET
Up from my cabin,
My sea-gown scarf'd about me, in the dark
Grop'd I to find out them: had my desire;
Finger'd their packet; and, in fine, withdrew
To mine own room again: making so bold,
My fears forgetting manners, to unseal
Their grand commission; where I found, Horatio,
O royal knavery! an exact command,—
Larded with many several sorts of reasons,
Importing Denmark's health, and England's too,
With, ho! such bugs and goblins in my life,—

That, on the supervise, no leisure bated,
No, not to stay the grinding of the axe,
My head should be struck off.

HORATIO
Is't possible?

HAMLET
Here's the commission: read it at more leisure.
But wilt thou bear me how I did proceed?

HORATIO
I beseech you.

HAMLET
Being thus benetted round with villanies,—
Or I could make a prologue to my brains,
They had begun the play,—I sat me down;
Devis'd a new commission; wrote it fair:
I once did hold it, as our statists do,
A baseness to write fair, and labour'd much
How to forget that learning; but, sir, now
It did me yeoman's service. Wilt thou know
The effect of what I wrote?

HORATIO
Ay, good my lord.

HAMLET
An earnest conjuration from the king,—
As England was his faithful tributary;
As love between them like the palm might flourish;
As peace should still her wheaten garland wear
And stand a comma 'tween their amities;
And many such-like as's of great charge,—
That, on the view and know of these contents,
Without debatement further, more or less,
He should the bearers put to sudden death,
Not shriving-time allow'd.

HORATIO
How was this seal'd?

HAMLET
Why, even in that was heaven ordinant.
I had my father's signet in my purse,
Which was the model of that Danish seal:
Folded the writ up in the form of the other;
Subscrib'd it: gave't the impression; plac'd it safely,
The changeling never known. Now, the next day
Was our sea-fight; and what to this was sequent
Thou know'st already.

HORATIO
So Guildenstern and Rosencrantz go to't.

HAMLET
Why, man, they did make love to this employment;
They are not near my conscience; their defeat
Does by their own insinuation grow:
'Tis dangerous when the baser nature comes
Between the pass and fell incensed points
Of mighty opposites.

HORATIO
Why, what a king is this!

HAMLET
Does it not, thinks't thee, stand me now upon,—
He that hath kill'd my king, and whor'd my mother;
Popp'd in between the election and my hopes;
Thrown out his angle for my proper life,
And with such cozenage—is't not perfect conscience
To quit him with this arm? and is't not to be damn'd
To let this canker of our nature come
In further evil?

HORATIO
It must be shortly known to him from England
What is the issue of the business there.

HAMLET
It will be short: the interim is mine;
And a man's life is no more than to say One.
But I am very sorry, good Horatio,
That to Laertes I forgot myself;
For by the image of my cause I see
The portraiture of his: I'll court his favours:
But, sure, the bravery of his grief did put me
Into a towering passion.

HORATIO
Peace; who comes here?

[Enter Osric.]

OSRIC
Your lordship is right welcome back to Denmark.

HAMLET
I humbly thank you, sir. Dost know this water-fly?
HORATIO
No, my good lord.

HAMLET
Thy state is the more gracious; for 'tis a vice to know him. He hath much land, and fertile: let a beast be lord of beasts, and his crib shall stand at the king's mess; 'tis a chough; but, as I say, spacious in the possession of dirt.

OSRIC
Sweet lord, if your lordship were at leisure, I should impart a thing to you from his majesty.

HAMLET
I will receive it with all diligence of spirit. Put your bonnet to his right use; 'tis for the head.

OSRIC
I thank your lordship, t'is very hot.

HAMLET
No, believe me, 'tis very cold; the wind is northerly.

OSRIC
It is indifferent cold, my lord, indeed.

HAMLET
Methinks it is very sultry and hot for my complexion.

OSRIC
Exceedingly, my lord; it is very sultry,—as 'twere—I cannot tell how. But, my lord, his majesty bade me signify to you that he has laid a great wager on your head. Sir, this is the matter,—

HAMLET
I beseech you, remember,—
[Hamlet moves him to put on his hat.]

OSRIC
Nay, in good faith; for mine ease, in good faith. Sir, here is newly come to court Laertes; believe me, an absolute gentleman, full of most excellent differences, of very soft society and great showing: indeed, to speak feelingly of him, he is the card or calendar of gentry; for you shall find in him the continent of what part a gentleman would see.

HAMLET
Sir, his definement suffers no perdition in you;—though, I know, to divide him inventorially would dizzy the arithmetic of memory, and yet but yaw neither, in respect of his quick sail. But, in the verity of extolment, I take him to be a soul of great article, and his infusion of such dearth and rareness as, to make true diction of him, his semblable is his mirror, and who else would trace him, his umbrage, nothing more.

OSRIC
Your lordship speaks most infallibly of him.

HAMLET
The concernancy, sir? why do we wrap the gentleman in our more rawer breath?

OSRIC
Sir?

HORATIO
Is't not possible to understand in another tongue? You will do't, sir, really.

HAMLET
What imports the nomination of this gentleman?

OSRIC
Of Laertes?

HORATIO
His purse is empty already; all's golden words are spent.

HAMLET
Of him, sir.

OSRIC
I know, you are not ignorant,—

HAMLET
I would you did, sir; yet, in faith, if you did, it would not much approve me.—Well, sir.

OSRIC
You are not ignorant of what excellence Laertes is,—

HAMLET
I dare not confess that, lest I should compare with him in excellence; but to know a man well were to know himself.

OSRIC
I mean, sir, for his weapon; but in the imputation laid on him by them, in his meed he's unfellowed.

HAMLET
What's his weapon?

OSRIC
Rapier and dagger.

HAMLET
That's two of his weapons:—but well.

OSRIC

The king, sir, hath wager'd with him six Barbary horses: against the which he has imponed, as I take it, six French rapiers and poniards, with their assigns, as girdle, hangers, and so: three of the carriages, in faith, are very dear to fancy, very responsive to the hilts, most delicate carriages, and of very liberal conceit.

HAMLET

What call you the carriages?

HORATIO

I knew you must be edified by the margent ere you had done.

OSRIC

The carriages, sir, are the hangers.

HAMLET

The phrase would be more german to the matter if we could carry cannon by our sides. I would it might be hangers till then. But, on: six Barbary horses against six French swords, their assigns, and three liberal conceited carriages: that's the French bet against the Danish: why is this all imponed, as you call it?

OSRIC

The king, sir, hath laid that, in a dozen passes between your and him, he shall not exceed you three hits: he hath laid on twelve for nine; and it would come to immediate trial if your lordship would vouchsafe the answer.

HAMLET

How if I answer no?

OSRIC

I mean, my lord, the opposition of your person in trial.

HAMLET

Sir, I will walk here in the hall: if it please his majesty, it is the breathing time of day with me: let the foils be brought, the gentleman willing, and the king hold his purpose, I will win for him if I can; if not, I will gain nothing but my shame and the odd hits.

OSRIC
Shall I re-deliver you e'en so?

HAMLET
To this effect, sir; after what flourish your nature will.

OSRIC
I commend my duty to your lordship.

HAMLET
Yours, yours.

[Exit Osric.]

He does well to commend it himself; there are no tongues else for's turn.

HORATIO
This lapwing runs away with the shell on his head.

HAMLET
He did comply with his dug before he suck'd it. Thus has he,— and many more of the same bevy that I know the drossy age dotes on,— only got the tune of the time and outward habit of encounter; a kind of yesty collection, which carries them through and through the most fanned and winnowed opinions; and do but blow them to their trial, the bubbles are out,

[Enter a Lord.]

LORD
My lord, his majesty commended him to you by young Osric, who brings back to him that you attend him in the hall: he sends to know if your pleasure hold to play with Laertes, or that you will take longer time.

HAMLET
I am constant to my purposes; they follow the king's pleasure: if his fitness speaks, mine is ready; now or whensoever, provided I be so able as now.

LORD
The King and Queen and all are coming down.

HAMLET
In happy time.

LORD
The queen desires you to use some gentle entertainment to Laertes
before you fall to play.

HAMLET
She well instructs me.

[Exit Lord.]

HORATIO
You will lose this wager, my lord.

HAMLET
I do not think so; since he went into France I have been in con-
tinual practice: I shall win at the odds. But thou wouldst not
think how ill all's here about my heart: but it is no matter.

HORATIO
Nay, good my lord,—

HAMLET
It is but foolery; but it is such a kind of gain-giving as would perhaps trouble a woman.

HORATIO
If your mind dislike anything, obey it: I will forestall their repair
hither, and say you are not fit.

HAMLET
Not a whit, we defy augury: there's a special providence in the fall
of a sparrow. If it be now, 'tis not to come; if it be not to come,
it will be now; if it be not now, yet it will come: the readiness is
all: since no man has aught of what he leaves, what is't to leave
betimes?

*[Enter King, Queen, Laertes, Lords, Osric, and Attendants with foils,
etc.]*

KING
Come, Hamlet, come, and take this hand from me.

[The King puts Laertes's hand into Hamlet's.]

HAMLET
Give me your pardon, sir: I have done you wrong:
But pardon't, as you are a gentleman.
This presence knows, and you must needs have heard,
How I am punish'd with sore distraction.
What I have done
That might your nature, honour, and exception
Roughly awake, I here proclaim was madness.
Was't Hamlet wrong'd Laertes? Never Hamlet:
If Hamlet from himself be ta'en away,
And when he's not himself does wrong Laertes,
Then Hamlet does it not, Hamlet denies it.
Who does it, then? His madness: if't be so,
Hamlet is of the faction that is wrong'd;
His madness is poor Hamlet's enemy.
Sir, in this audience,
Let my disclaiming from a purpos'd evil
Free me so far in your most generous thoughts
That I have shot my arrow o'er the house
And hurt my brother.

LAERTES
I am satisfied in nature,
Whose motive, in this case, should stir me most
To my revenge. But in my terms of honour
I stand aloof; and will no reconcilement
Till by some elder masters of known honour
I have a voice and precedent of peace
To keep my name ungor'd. But till that time
I do receive your offer'd love like love,
And will not wrong it.

HAMLET
I embrace it freely;
And will this brother's wager frankly play.—
Give us the foils; come on.

LAERTES
Come, one for me.

HAMLET
I'll be your foil, Laertes; in mine ignorance
Your skill shall, like a star in the darkest night,
Stick fiery off indeed.

LAERTES
You mock me, sir.

HAMLET
No, by this hand.

KING
Give them the foils, young Osric. Cousin Hamlet,
You know the wager?

HAMLET
Very well, my lord;
Your grace has laid the odds o' the weaker side.

KING
I do not fear it; I have seen you both;
But since he's better'd, we have therefore odds.

LAERTES
This is too heavy, let me see another.

HAMLET
This likes me well. These foils have all a length?

[They prepare to play.]

OSRIC
Ay, my good lord.

KING
Set me the stoups of wine upon that table,—
If Hamlet give the first or second hit,
Or quit in answer of the third exchange,
Let all the battlements their ordnance fire;
The king shall drink to Hamlet's better breath;
And in the cup an union shall he throw,
Richer than that which four successive kings
In Denmark's crown have worn. Give me the cups;
And let the kettle to the trumpet speak,
The trumpet to the cannoneer without,
The cannons to the heavens, the heavens to earth,
'Now the king drinks to Hamlet.'—Come, begin:—
And you, the judges, bear a wary eye.

HAMLET
Come on, sir.

LAERTES
Come, my lord.

[They play.]

HAMLET
One.

LAERTES
No.

HAMLET
Judgment!

OSRIC
A hit, a very palpable hit.

LAERTES
Well;—again.

KING
Stay, give me drink.—Hamlet, this pearl is thine;
Here's to thy health.—

[Trumpets sound, and cannon shot off within.]

Give him the cup.

HAMLET
I'll play this bout first; set it by awhile.—
Come.—Another hit; what say you?

[They play.]

LAERTES
A touch, a touch, I do confess.

KING
Our son shall win.

QUEEN
He's fat, and scant of breath.—
Here, Hamlet, take my napkin, rub thy brows:
The queen carouses to thy fortune, Hamlet.

HAMLET
Good madam!

KING
Gertrude, do not drink.
QUEEN
I will, my lord; I pray you pardon me.

KING
[Aside.] It is the poison'd cup; it is too late.

HAMLET
I dare not drink yet, madam; by-and-by.

QUEEN
Come, let me wipe thy face.

LAERTES
My lord, I'll hit him now.

KING
I do not think't.

LAERTES
[Aside.] And yet 'tis almost 'gainst my conscience.

HAMLET
Come, for the third, Laertes: you but dally;
I pray you pass with your best violence:
I am afeard you make a wanton of me.

LAERTES
Say you so? come on.

[They play.]

OSRIC
Nothing, neither way.

LAERTES
Have at you now!

[Laertes wounds Hamlet; then, in scuffling, they change rapiers, and Hamlet wounds Laertes.]

KING
Part them; they are incens'd.

HAMLET
Nay, come again!
[The Queen falls.]

OSRIC
Look to the queen there, ho!

HORATIO
They bleed on both sides.—How is it, my lord?

OSRIC
How is't, Laertes?

LAERTES
Why, as a woodcock to my own springe, Osric;
I am justly kill'd with mine own treachery.

HAMLET
How does the queen?

KING
She swoons to see them bleed.

QUEEN
No, no! the drink, the drink!—O my dear Hamlet!—
The drink, the drink!—I am poison'd.

[Dies.]

HAMLET
O villany!—Ho! let the door be lock'd:
Treachery! seek it out.

[Laertes falls.]

LAERTES
It is here, Hamlet: Hamlet, thou art slain;
No medicine in the world can do thee good;
In thee there is not half an hour of life;
The treacherous instrument is in thy hand,
Unbated and envenom'd: the foul practice
Hath turn'd itself on me; lo, here I lie,
Never to rise again: thy mother's poison'd:
I can no more:—the king, the king's to blame.

HAMLET
The point envenom'd too!—
Then, venom, to thy work.

[Stabs the King.]

OSRIC AND LORDS
Treason! treason!

KING
O, yet defend me, friends! I am but hurt.

HAMLET
Here, thou incestuous, murderous, damned Dane,
Drink off this potion.—Is thy union here?
Follow my mother.

[King dies.]

LAERTES
He is justly serv'd;
It is a poison temper'd by himself.—
Exchange forgiveness with me, noble Hamlet:
Mine and my father's death come not upon thee,
Nor thine on me!

[Dies.]

HAMLET
Heaven make thee free of it! I follow thee.—
I am dead, Horatio.—Wretched queen, adieu!—
You that look pale and tremble at this chance,
That are but mutes or audience to this act,
Had I but time,—as this fell sergeant, death,
Is strict in his arrest,—O, I could tell you,—
But let it be.—Horatio, I am dead;
Thou liv'st; report me and my cause aright
To the unsatisfied.

HORATIO
Never believe it:
I am more an antique Roman than a Dane.—
Here's yet some liquor left.

HAMLET
As thou'rt a man,
Give me the cup; let go; by heaven, I'll have't.—
O good Horatio, what a wounded name,
Things standing thus unknown, shall live behind me!
If thou didst ever hold me in thy heart,
Absent thee from felicity awhile,
And in this harsh world draw thy breath in pain,
To tell my story.—

[March afar off, and shot within.]

What warlike noise is this?

Osric
Young Fortinbras, with conquest come from Poland,
To the ambassadors of England gives
This warlike volley.

Hamlet
O, I die, Horatio;
The potent poison quite o'er-crows my spirit:
I cannot live to hear the news from England;
But I do prophesy the election lights
On Fortinbras: he has my dying voice;
So tell him, with the occurrents, more and less,
Which have solicited.—the rest is silence.

[Dies.]

Horatio
Now cracks a noble heart.—Good night, sweet prince,
And flights of angels sing thee to thy rest!
Why does the drum come hither?

[March within.]

[Enter Fortinbras, the English Ambassadors, and others.]

Fortinbras
Where is this sight?

Horatio
What is it you will see?
If aught of woe or wonder, cease your search.

Fortinbras
This quarry cries on havoc.—O proud death,
What feast is toward in thine eternal cell,
That thou so many princes at a shot
So bloodily hast struck?

1 Ambassador
The sight is dismal;
And our affairs from England come too late:

The ears are senseless that should give us hearing,
To tell him his commandment is fulfill'd
That Rosencrantz and Guildenstern are dead:
Where should we have our thanks?

HORATIO
Not from his mouth,
Had it the ability of life to thank you:
He never gave commandment for their death.
But since, so jump upon this bloody question,
You from the Polack wars, and you from England,
Are here arriv'd, give order that these bodies
High on a stage be placed to the view;
And let me speak to the yet unknowing world
How these things came about: so shall you hear
Of carnal, bloody and unnatural acts;
Of accidental judgments, casual slaughters;
Of deaths put on by cunning and forc'd cause;
And, in this upshot, purposes mistook
Fall'n on the inventors' heads: all this can I
Truly deliver.

FORTINBRAS
Let us haste to hear it,
And call the noblest to the audience.
For me, with sorrow I embrace my fortune:
I have some rights of memory in this kingdom,
Which now, to claim my vantage doth invite me.

HORATIO
Of that I shall have also cause to speak,
And from his mouth whose voice will draw on more:
But let this same be presently perform'd,
Even while men's minds are wild: lest more mischance
On plots and errors happen.

FORTINBRAS

Let four captains

Bear Hamlet like a soldier to the stage;

For he was likely, had he been put on,

To have prov'd most royally: and, for his passage,

The soldiers' music and the rites of war

Speak loudly for him.—

Take up the bodies.—Such a sight as this

Becomes the field, but here shows much amiss.

Go, bid the soldiers shoot.

[A dead march.]

[Exeunt, bearing off the dead bodies; after which a peal of ordnance is shot off.]

END

Made in the USA
San Bernardino, CA
30 October 2015